**Six winners. Six fantasies.
Six skeletons come out of the closet...**

Plain Jane Kurtz is going to use her winnings to discover her inner vixen. But what's it *really* going to cost her?

New girl in town Nicole Reavis is on a journey to find herself. But what *else* will she discover along the way?

Risk-taker Eve Best is on the verge of having everything she's ever wanted. But can she take it?

Young, cocky Zach Haas loves his instant popularity, especially with the women. But can he trust it?

Solid, dependable Cole Crawford is ready to shake things up. But how "shook up" is he prepared to handle?

Wild child Liza Skinner has always just wanted to belong. But how far is she willing to go to get it?

Million Dollar Secrets—do you feel lucky?

Blaze™

Dear Reader,

Most of you probably know that this is the final book in the MILLION DOLLAR SECRETS miniseries. I loved writing this story. Liza is one of my favorite heroines ever. For an author, a continuity is a little different, in that the general stories are predetermined—meaning not author generated—as part of the bigger picture. I admit that when I first read that Liza was supposed to sue her friends, I was turned off and didn't know how I could write such a character. How could I bond with a woman like that? Or make her sympathetic to readers?

The hero, Evan, came to the rescue. He's perfect in every way and I really wanted Liza to deserve him. I wanted him to be perfect for her, too. She needed someone stable and patient, with a good sense of humor. She deserved someone who would accept her unconditionally. Evan has his own baggage to lose, as well. He needed Liza as much as she did him. And when they finally let go, magic happened.

I hope you enjoy their story.

Debbi Rawlins

DEBBI RAWLINS

What She *Really* Wants for Christmas

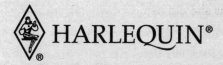

HARLEQUIN®

TORONTO • NEW YORK • LONDON
AMSTERDAM • PARIS • SYDNEY • HAMBURG
STOCKHOLM • ATHENS • TOKYO • MILAN • MADRID
PRAGUE • WARSAW • BUDAPEST • AUCKLAND

ISBN-13: 978-0-373-79372-3
ISBN-10:   0-373-79372-3

WHAT SHE *REALLY* WANTS FOR CHRISTMAS

www.eHarlequin.com

Printed in U.S.A.

ABOUT THE AUTHOR

Debbi Rawlins lives in central Utah, out in the country, surrounded by woods and deer and wild turkeys. It's quite a change for a city girl who didn't even know where the state of Utah was until four years ago. Of course, unfamiliarity never stopped her. Between her junior and senior years of college she spontaneously left home in Hawaii and bummed around Europe for five weeks by herself. And much to her parents' delight, returned home with only a quarter in her wallet.

Books by Debbi Rawlins

Don't miss any of our special offers. Write to us at the following address for information on our newest releases.

Harlequin Reader Service
U.S.: 3010 Walden Ave., P.O. Box 1325, Buffalo, NY 14269
Canadian: P.O. Box 609, Fort Erie, Ont. L2A 5X3

1

Rumor has it that Atlanta's own *Just Between Us,* the three-year-old, sex-themed, hot-topic afternoon television show hosted by Eve Best, is soon going into national syndication. Geared toward women's perspectives and concerns, the local show has garnered a widely growing audience and advertisers have taken notice. While taking on contemporary, cutting-edge topics, Ms. Best's energy and spontaneity has captured the attention of teens and mothers alike.

Recently, however, the local show has drawn a maelstrom of not-so-flattering publicity. Most of you already know about the state lottery win, shared by six employees of the show, including Ms. Best. But what this reporter has just learned is that despite attempts to keep the unpleasantness quiet, a lawsuit filed by a former segment producer, Liza Skinner, has halted the disbursement of the winnings.

According to my source, Ms. Skinner was

an original member of the lottery pool before
leaving the show nearly a year ago. There is
some confusion as to whether she still had
money in the pot, but the number 13, which
she'd chosen, was among the six winning
numbers, and apparently she seems to think
she deserves a share.

LIZA QUIT READING the article and threw the copy
of last week's *Atlanta Daily News* onto the passenger seat of her compact car. When she got home,
she was throwing the tattered paper away. No use
continuing to torture herself. The wheels were
already in motion. Soon it would all be over. She
hoped.

She pushed a shaky hand through her tangled
hair and tried to get comfortable—not easy with her
long legs. She had no business being here. Her
attorney had told her to stay away from the *Just
Between Us* studio. At least until her lawsuit was
settled. Of course then there'd be no reason to be
here, in the parking lot, waiting, like a smitten
schoolgirl, for a glimpse of Eve and Jane. No
matter which way the suit went, her friends would
never speak to her again.

She didn't blame them. All she'd done in the past
year was cause them pain. Hadn't they warned her
about Rick? From the start, they knew he'd be
trouble. They'd been her best friends since the sixth
grade, closer to her than anyone in the whole world.
Why hadn't she listened to them?

Liza let her head fall back against the worn cloth upholstery and forced herself to breathe. He'd been just her type, wild and sexy and a little dangerous, and she'd thought he was the one. He turned out to be way more dangerous than she'd ever imagined.

Movement caught her eye and she turned her head just in time to see a woman step outside, the sunlight glimmering off her pale-blond hair. She looked like Nicole, the *Just Between Us* segment producer who'd replaced Liza. The woman who was going to get Liza's share of the lottery money. Unless the lawsuit was successful.

God, why didn't they just pay up? It wasn't as if each of them wasn't going to still be filthy rich after coughing up her share. She closed her eyes, blocking out the image of the woman walking toward a red convertible. A reminder of how much Liza had lost. Just another month and it would all be over.

Although, if she had the guts, she could go to Eve and Jane now. Confess everything. The idea took hold and her breathing quickened. Slowly, she opened her eyes. Could it be that simple? After nearly a year of selling her soul? Ha. Sure, confessing would ease her conscience, but that wouldn't solve anything. Eve would still be vulnerable to public humiliation. And it would still be Liza's fault.

She hung her head and stared at her pitiful cuticles. Nowadays she couldn't even afford a manicure. The small inheritance she'd received after her father's death last year was nearly gone and there was rent to pay, attorney's fees and a myriad of other things. But what she resented the most was the money Rick spent on cigarettes, booze and drugs. Money she could've used to buy a better car, live in a better neighborhood.

Maybe when this was over she'd be able to find a decent job. Never one like she had with *Just Between Us*. That had been a dream job. The once-in-a-lifetime kind. She knew because she'd been a part of it from the beginning. Those crazy, fifteen-hour days when none of them knew what they were doing, but they pushed forward, tackling any task they were given, their passion making up for what they'd lacked in experience.

Their hard work had paid off. The show was a huge success. This should have been the best time in Liza's life. But she was no longer a part of her friends' lives or a part of the show. All because of her stupidity. Even if Eve and Jane eventually forgave her, she seriously doubted she could forgive herself.

Eve walked out of the redbrick building, and Liza bit down on her lower lip. The radiance in her friend's face made Liza's stomach knot. Behind her was the reason for Eve's glow. Tall and good-looking, with dark hair, the man put a familiar hand at the small of Eve's back.

Liza had heard Eve had found someone, Mitch Hayes, the guy who had once represented the television network wanting to sign *Just Between Us*. She looked happy. Happier than Liza had ever seen her.

Damn. No way was Liza getting her friends

involved now. She'd push for the settlement, pay off Rick and then she'd disappear. Start a new life where no one knew her, where she wouldn't be considered scum of the earth.

And never see her friends again.

Liza squeezed her eyes shut, willing the threatening tears away. At least Eve would be spared any humiliation. A tear escaped and, angry, Liza swiped at it. Crying wouldn't solve a damn thing. Never had. Never would. She scrubbed at her eyes, disgusted at the display of weakness.

And then she heard something. Knocking. At the car window.

Opening her eyes, she swung her face toward the sound. A man with short dark hair and concerned brown eyes stared back at her. It took a moment to recognize him…the doctor who consulted for the medical drama shot in the studio next to *Just Between Us*. Dr. Evan something. He'd asked her to lunch once. She'd blown him off. Sedate and conservative. Definitely not her type.

She took another furtive swipe at her eyes, annoyed that he might have seen her crying. When he motioned for her to let down her window, she was tempted to ignore him. But that was bound to make matters worse, and the last thing she needed was a scene in front of the station.

Lucky she could afford a car at all, she didn't have the luxury of automatic windows and manually rolled it down. He ducked through, gripping the top of the door, and smiled. She didn't.

"Liza, hi." He paused. "Remember me?"

She deliberately frowned and gave a small shake of her head. If the slight embarrassed him, maybe he'd leave her alone.

"Evan Gann." He inclined his head toward the building. "From the studio beside *Just Between Us.*"

"Oh, right. You're the consultant."

He nodded, his eyes probing. "I haven't seen you for a while."

"I'm persona non grata around here. Surely, you've heard."

"Ah, the lawsuit." His eyebrows drew together. "I don't know the details—"

"You wanted something?"

His mouth curved in an annoyingly tolerant smile. "I was surprised to see you. Look, you want to have a drink sometime?"

"Why?"

He chuckled. "Because you're attractive and I like you?"

It took Liza a moment to collect herself. Was this guy nuts? He'd probably be banned from the station just for talking to her. She frowned. Except he really wasn't nuts. He was this straightlaced, normal kind of guy. "I've got too much going on right now." She reached for the knob to roll up the window, and when he didn't move, she said, "Do you mind?"

"Why don't you take my number for when you have some time? I'll buy you dinner."

"Look, Evan, you're a nice guy but—"

"Thought you didn't remember me?" His slow, teasing grin did something to the inside of her chest.

She almost smiled. "See you around," she said, and this time when she attempted to roll up the window, he let go and stepped back. She started the engine, reversed out of the parking spot and drove off without looking back.

EVAN REACHED INTO his slacks' pocket for his car keys and used the remote to unlock the doors. His silver Camry was parked right next to the spot Liza had vacated. That was the only reason he'd noticed her, sitting behind the wheel of the small white compact, crying. Wisely, he hadn't mentioned it. From what he knew of her, she wasn't the type of woman who indulged herself with tears. In fact, from what he'd heard around the station, she'd been more prone to express her anger or pain with a few choice words.

Still, the lawsuit she'd launched didn't add up. Until a year ago, Liza, Eve and Jane had been inseparable. He'd admired their loyalty and friendship. The show was really taking off, thanks to Eve Best's charismatic personality and Liza's creative genius. And then suddenly Liza disappeared. No one seemed to know why she left or where she went, and he had to admit, he was a bit curious.

Mostly because he'd liked Liza from the first time he'd met her. He'd been on his way to the set of *Heartbeat* when he'd bumped into her. Literally.

She'd been talking to someone over her shoulder and hadn't seen him come around the corner. Abruptly she'd turned and plowed right into him. Unfortunately for him, she'd been holding a cup of coffee.

He smiled when he thought about how she'd tried to right the wrong, using her napkin to blot his suit, regardless of where the coffee had landed. When she'd finally realized that pressing the napkin to his crotch might not have been the wisest move, she'd looked him in the eye, apologized and asked to be given the cleaning bill.

No nervous twittering or inane remarks. She wasn't like so many of the women he met, either on the set or at dinner parties hosted by his well-intentioned friends, who were determined to find him a wife. Liza was straightforward, to the point, and he liked that. Normally he preferred petite blondes, which made his attraction to her all the more curious, since she was tall with long, unruly brown hair.

Not that it mattered. He'd asked Liza out to lunch once, and in her no-nonsense fashion, she'd turned him down flat. No excuses, no little white lies to let him down easy. Just a frank refusal that told him not to ask again. After that there was the occasional exchange of greetings when they passed each other in the lobby or parking lot.

Realizing he was still staring after her long-gone car, he opened the door of his Camry and slid behind the wheel. Eve had walked out of the building ahead of him, but obviously she wasn't the reason Liza had been here. So why was she here? More importantly, why did he care? She'd just shot him down again.

IT WAS SO LATE by the time Liza got home that there wasn't a single parking spot left in the complex and she had to park a block away from her apartment. Sighing, she cut the car's engine and then grabbed the bag of burgers she'd picked up from a drive-through. She really hated parking on the street, especially in this crappy neighborhood. Hopefully, any thieves would go for the nice new black sedan parked in front of her.

Not that she loved her secondhand lemon of a car. But if something happened to it, she couldn't afford to buy another one. Rick had naturally insisted on buying a brand-new Harley-Davidson for himself. With her money. Amazing he hadn't cracked it up yet. Not that it would hurt her feelings if he had. In fact, in her more stressed-out moments, she'd actually wished he would. He didn't have to die or anything, just end up in a coma for a good five years.

Her steps slowed as she thought about how he lived in the apartment right next to hers, and that if he happened to look out of the window he'd see her walk up the stairs. Inevitably he'd come outside and grill her about where she'd been. His language would be foul and he wouldn't give a damn about who overheard. But if she was lucky, he'd be passed out and she wouldn't have to deal with him until tomorrow.

Sighing, she took the first few stairs, her daze darting toward Rick's door, praying, hoping she'd have an evening of peace and quiet. So far, so good…

"Hey, Liza, what you got in the bag?"

The sound of her new neighbor's high-pitched voice made Liza cringe. She waved for Mary Ellen to keep it down and then, with one eye on Rick's door, she hurried the rest of the way to the third floor.

Leaning over the railing, which was decorated with a string of large colored Christmas lights, Mary Ellen waited, dutifully keeping her mouth shut until Liza joined her. "I think he's passed out," the younger woman said in that strange drawl of hers.

She claimed that she and her kid were from Mississippi but Liza had her doubts. The apartment complex's residents weren't exactly members of mainstream society. At least once a week Liza heard a shot fired nearby, or watched the police drag away an abusive husband or boyfriend. But the rent was cheap and since she had to fork out money for both her place and Rick's, this was the best she could afford.

Rick thought it was stupid to have separate apartments, mostly because he wanted complete control over her. But that was the one thing she wouldn't negotiate with him. She didn't care that she'd end up broke, but as threadbare as it was, her sanity wasn't something she was ready to give up. Bad enough that he tried to keep track of her every move, she sure didn't need him in her face.

She reached the third-floor landing and furtively peeked into Rick's open window. Sure enough, he lay flat on his back on the tattered brown corduroy couch that they'd picked up at a thrift store. An empty bottle of vodka sat on the end table, but she knew he'd consumed more than booze. Good. Maybe she could have a quiet meal with Mary Ellen and her daughter.

"Told ya." Mary Ellen inclined her dirty-blond head toward Rick's apartment, but her gaze stayed on the fast-food bag.

"Hungry?"

"Starving."

"I bought extra burgers for you and Freedom."

Mary Ellen broke into a wide grin that displayed a missing back tooth, which wasn't usually noticeable since she didn't smile much. "Oh, goody. I thought we were gonna have to eat macaroni and cheese again." She turned around, put two fingers into her mouth and let out an ear-piercing whistle.

Liza cringed. With dread, she took a step back and squinted into Rick's apartment. He was still out cold. However, Freedom heard her mom's whistle and came bounding up the stairs.

"Hi, Liza." The eight-year-old tomboy was covered with dirt. She pulled off her red ball cap and dust flew everywhere.

"Time for dinner?" she asked her mom, her hopeful blue eyes going to the bag.

"Liza bought us burgers."

"Yahoo. Fries, too?"

Liza unlocked her apartment door. "They would've gotten cold."

"The hamburgers are cold, too," Freedom said, with perfect logic.

"That's true," Mary Ellen said, her slight frown accentuating the scar paralleling her lower lip.

Sighing, Liza led them inside and went straight to the microwave. Eating cold French fries wasn't the same thing, but Liza didn't want to get into it with them. She wanted them to eat and leave. In fact, she should've given them the food to take back to their own apartment, but she had a soft spot for Mary Ellen and her daughter.

As pitiful as Liza's place was with its chipped paint and stained, olive-green carpet, the other two managed to live in a cheaper, cramped studio apartment. Mary Ellen still ended up two months behind on the rent since her welfare checks didn't quite cover all their expenses. With her pronounced limp, she'd had trouble finding a job that would support the two of them. Liza had never asked her about the bum leg, but she had a bad feeling about it.

She finished nuking the burgers and Mary Ellen had already put napkins on the small table. It was only big enough for two, so Freedom sat on her mother's good knee. She quickly wolfed down her burger, and eyed a second one. Liza pushed it across to her, wishing she'd bought more than five sandwiches. When Mary Ellen finished hers, Liza offered her the last one.

"What about Rick?"

Amazing how just the mention of him could knot her stomach and send the hair straight up off the back of her neck. "What about him?"

"Isn't he eating?"

"Don't know. Don't care."

Mary Ellen regarded her quizzically. "Why do you stay with him?"

"I'm not *with* him." Liza grabbed the used wrappers and crumpled them as she got to her feet. She'd seen the curious looks Mary Ellen had given her on the unfortunate occasions when Rick was drunk and he'd yelled from the door of his apartment as Liza was trying to slip quietly down the stairs. But she didn't intend to discuss her problems with Mary Ellen. Or anyone else.

"Why do you live next door to him, then?" the other woman asked.

Liza disposed of the wrappers, using the time to compose herself. Anyone else and she would have told them it was none of their damn business, but having to look into Mary Ellen's perpetually sad eyes, Liza just couldn't do it.

"It's complicated," she said finally.

"That means you don't want to talk about it, huh?" the little girl mumbled, her mouth full.

"Freedom," Mary Ellen admonished her. "This is grown-up talk. You be quiet."

Liza hid a smile. Poor kid was going to grow up to be like her. Smart-mouthed and always in trouble.

"You went to college, didn't you?" Mary Ellen asked.

Liza slowly nodded, not liking the conversation.

"You're so pretty and smart and I don't understand why you'd be living in a dump like this."

Right. Real smart. So smart that she'd put herself in a position to be blackmailed. "Look," Liza said in a tight voice, casting a brief glance at Freedom, who'd turned to licking her fingers instead of listening to the conversation. "I don't think you want to start a question-and-answer session."

Mary Ellen looked grimly down at her weather-roughened hands. "No," she said quietly, and then cleared her throat and rose from the table. "Freedom, come on. We need to be going. Thanks for dinner, Liza." She pulled her daughter along with her, keeping her face toward the door.

"See you later." Liza stayed in the small open kitchen and watched them go. She probably should've made nice. Mary Ellen hadn't meant anything bad by what she'd said. The woman seemed to have such a lonely life, likely she only wanted to talk.

But Liza didn't have it in her. Not today. Everything had gone wrong. After being decisive all of her life, she'd become as stable as a palm tree in a hurricane. She should never have allowed the blackmail to get this far, but she'd panicked and everything had spiraled out of control before she knew what had happened. Winning the lawsuit would save her ass, if she could only keep her act together.

She walked to the love seat and sank down, careful to avoid the bad spring in the center. God, was this headache ever going away? She leaned forward, rested her elbows on her knees and cradled her head in her hands. She needed a couple of aspirin. But that meant leaving to get them. No way. She was staying right where she was to enjoy the peace and quiet while Rick was passed out.

Going to the station had been a bad idea. She'd known it before she'd gotten in the car. But that was the sort of stupid irrational behavior she couldn't seem to control anymore. Even though she'd never made it out of her car. Thanks to Evan Gann. People didn't know how to mind their own damn business.

If she'd gotten into the studio, she might have learned whether another settlement was being considered. The last offer they'd made, Rick had flatly refused. Although since she'd pumped Zach Hass, the new guy, for information, everyone named in the lawsuit had probably been warned not to talk to her. For all she knew, security wouldn't even have let her inside. Unless...

She abruptly brought her head up.

Evan Gann. He could get her inside. No one could stop her if she was going to see him. Damn it. Why hadn't she taken his phone number? Grudgingly she pushed to her feet, and got her cell phone. She hoped like hell his number was listed.

2

AT THREE FORTY-FIVE Evan took a few minutes away
from the set and called his office and then his answering service. Because of the consulting job, he
only saw patients three days a week, but inevitably,
on the rare occasion that he wanted some personal
time, there'd be an emergency that would consume
the rest of his day. Fortunately, this afternoon he
was free to see Liza.

What a shock it had been when she'd called last
night. As a result he'd been on edge all day. It
seemed as if every shot had gone wrong and there'd
been so many retakes that he was afraid he
wouldn't be done when she arrived at four fifteen.
He'd finally had to pull the assistant director aside
and tell her that he was going to be out of here by
four, no matter what.

The truth was, his concentration wasn't what it
should be anyway. He didn't get why Liza had
decided to see him. No sign she'd been interested
yesterday. So why the sudden change of heart? And
why did she want to meet him at the studio? Strange
that she'd want to show her face here at all.

Even stranger that he was still interested in her. Especially this time of the year. Ever since medical school and the Angela debacle, he had no use for the holidays. So what was it about Liza? He couldn't quite grasp the attraction. Had to be something chemical. Pheromones, maybe. Or maybe that he was a sucker for a crying woman. He had an annoying urge to rescue them.

He checked his watch and saw that the AD had noticed. She gave him a small nod and he didn't think twice before grabbing his jacket and heading off the set. He was early but he kept an electric razor in his car's glove box. He could barely make it through the day without dark stubble covering his chin.

He'd made it halfway through the lobby when he heard the receptionist call out his name. Melinda wasn't at her usual station but was decorating a Christmas tree in the corner. She was blond, petite and pretty, and she wasn't shy about making her interest in him known. But she was too young and a little too brazen for his taste. Besides, she reminded him of his ex-fiancée.

"You're right on time, Evan," she said brightly, holding a glittering star and standing on a short ladder. "I can't reach the top." She demonstrated by stretching so high that pretty much everyone in the lobby noticed that she wore pink lacy underwear.

Evan kept his eyes on her face as he stayed en route to the double doors. "Where's Leroy?" The ex-basketball-player-turned-security-guard wouldn't even need the ladder.

"I don't know," she said petulantly. "Can't you help me?"

"I'm running late." He hesitated and glanced out the glass doors. "All right."

She smiled and handed him the star before slowly descending the ladder, with a seductive sway to her curvy hips.

The tree had to be eight feet tall and since he was only six-two he didn't dare try securing the star without using the ladder. He got up a couple of rungs and felt Melinda's hand near his right thigh. He frowned down at her.

"I'm holding the ladder for you," she said with a wink.

He ignored her, placed the star on the top of the tree and then quickly got down.

"You're leaving early." The woman had no concept of personal space.

He backed away from her, at the same time glancing out the glass doors. He spotted Liza pulling into a parking space. "I've got to go."

"You have a date or something?" she asked in a teasing tone.

"Yeah," he said, and headed out of the building without giving her a second look.

The sky was darker and the air chillier than when he'd come to work midmorning. He buttoned his jacket as he walked, watching for Liza, his gaze staying on the large black SUV she'd parked behind. A second later he saw her, dressed in jeans and a bulky red sweater that unfortunately hid her curves. He waved to get her attention.

"What are you doing out here?" she asked as soon as she got close enough.

Evan checked his watch. "Weren't we supposed to meet at four fifteen?"

Resentment flashed in her eyes. "Too embarrassed to be seen with me inside?"

"Never even crossed my mind. I was done, and I walked out here to meet you. Is that a problem?"

Her gaze flickered toward the station doors. "No."

"Shall we take my car?"

"I guess."

He didn't appreciate her indifferent tone. "Look, if you've changed your mind, no problem."

Liza shook her head. "No, I'm sorry. I'd like to have a drink with you. Anyplace. You choose."

Evan tried not to smile. Originally she'd asked him just to go for coffee, which was okay because he'd considered it a nice start. A drink was better. Maybe it would even lead to dinner. "How about we go to Sardis?"

"That's a couple blocks away, isn't it?"

He nodded.

"Let's walk."

"You're not cold?"

Liza laughed. Nice husky sound. "It's only the beginning of December. Ask me next month."

Would she still be around then? Naturally he said nothing. He simply walked alongside her, and when they got to the sidewalk, promptly swung around to take the outside position closer to the street.

Her lips lifted in amusement. "A perfect Southern gentleman, I see."

He shrugged sheepishly. "My grandfather once made me promise to never let a woman walk on the street side. Do you know how the custom came about?"

"Ah, no."

Evan smiled. He could tell she didn't care but she was going to hear it anyway. "It started back in the old west. Unpaved roads, puddles of water... you starting to get the picture?"

She shook her head in mock disgust, but he saw the smile dancing at the corners of her mouth.

"A gentleman always walked on the outside to protect the women from getting their long skirts splashed."

She laughed, making her eyes sparkle. She wasn't classically pretty but she had an interesting face. Her eyes were small and almond-shaped, and her nose looked as if it had been sculpted by a skilled surgeon. Although she didn't strike him as a woman who'd go in for that kind of thing.

He smiled. "And now you know."

"Is that true?"

"I have no idea."

Her eyebrows arched. "You made it up?"

"No, I heard it from my grandfather. I imagine he did read it somewhere, though. I remember him always reading a book or newspaper."

She looked away. "I don't remember my grand-parents. I was a baby when they died."

"All four of them?"

"Yeah," she said, showing undue interest in the Santa window display they were passing.

He got that it might be a sore subject and dropped it. "You look nice."

She gave him an annoyed look. "This is a drink, okay? You're not getting lucky."

"No problem. I'm celibate." As much as he wanted to see Liza's expression, he had to look away because he had a lousy poker face.

Fortunately, at that moment they arrived at the bar, both of them going for the door, but he got it first. He held it open for her.

"Celibate and a gentleman. This is going to be interesting," she murmured as she proceeded him.

Evan followed her, disturbed by the new view he was getting. The sweater wasn't hiding any curves. She'd lost a lot of weight. About twenty pounds that she hadn't needed to lose. Was she sick? Was that the reason for her sudden disappearance? Is that why she needed the lottery money?

The light vanilla fragrance of her hair distracted him, and drew him closer than was polite. When she stopped suddenly, he nearly rammed into her. She turned to say something and their eyes met. She didn't look pleased.

"There's a table over there," he said, discreetly backing up a foot.

She hesitated, her gaze turning toward the dimly

lit room, the walls covered with racing memorabilia and autographed pictures. Artificial garlands interwoven with Christmas lights were draped along the heavy wooden bar. A Christmas tree stood in the corner but it hadn't been decorated yet. There were a lot of customers for the time of day, talking and laughing or thoughtfully sipping their cocktails.

Evan only recognized one person who worked at the station—a cameraman from another show that was filmed down the hall. Luckily, he had nothing to do with *Just Between Us* and he was probably new enough that Liza wouldn't recognize him.

"This okay?" he asked close to her ear.

"This is fine. I could do without all the damn decorations but I don't think we can get away from that."

"Don't like Christmas, huh?"

"Not particularly."

"Me, neither."

She looked at him with surprise but a couple came in behind them and since there were only two available tables, he and Liza headed toward the one he'd spotted in the corner. It hadn't been cleaned off yet from the previous customers and a waitress promptly removed the empty glasses, wiped off the tabletop with a towel and then said she'd be back to take their drink orders.

After a brief but awkward silence, Evan spoke first. "You can tell me to go to hell, but I'm going to ask the burning question. Where have you been for the last year?"

Liza leaned back in her chair and stared at him. "Does it matter?"

That, he hadn't expected. "I guess not."

"Good." A hint of a smile played at the corners of her mouth. "Now I don't have to tell you to go to hell."

"Go ahead. I can take it. I've got broad shoulders."

"Do you now?" She gave him an obvious once-over. "I see that you do."

"Careful or I'll think you're flirting with me."

She laughed. "I wouldn't do that to a man in your condition."

Now that he thought about it, he was painfully close to celibacy. His nurse thought he was too picky. "How thoughtful."

Liza opened her mouth to say something and then closed it again when their waitress appeared. The woman waited patiently while Liza changed her mind twice about what she wanted to drink. Finally, she settled on a tequila sunrise with an extra cherry. Surprising, because he'd expected her to drink something like scotch or beer.

After he'd given his order and the waitress left, he waited for Liza to pick up the conversation again, but when she didn't, he asked, "What have you been doing with yourself?"

She looked uncomfortable, shifting in her seat and feigning interest in the picture of a Grand Prix racing crew on the wall. "Nothing much."

"You have a job?"

"I'm looking."

"In the same field?"

"Why so many questions?" she snapped.

"Well, let's see, I suppose we could talk about the weather."

Liza sighed. "I really don't know what I'm going to do yet."

"Waiting for the lawsuit to play out, I imagine."

She flinched. "It's not about the money."

"Oh?" Jeez, he really was just making conversation.

She moistened her lips. "Have you heard anything?"

"You mean, around the station?"

She slowly nodded, her anxious hazel eyes staying fastened on his.

He chuckled. "Your name has popped up from time to time."

"I know they all think I'm a bitch."

"I wouldn't say that."

Her chin went up in defiance. "You don't have to protect my tender feelings. I really don't give a damn."

"I know. I was talking about the janitor. He doesn't speak English, so I doubt he has an opinion of you."

Liza grinned. "Very good, Dr. Gann."

"Why, thank you." Silly how good it felt to have impressed Liza. But mostly it was about how her face relaxed when she smiled. How pretty she looked.

"Here we go." The waitress set the tequila

sunrise in front of Liza along with a small white bowl of maraschino cherries. She put a bottle of imported beer in front of Evan, and then another bowl of pretzels in the center of the table.

"Thank you." Liza looked at the waitress, an odd expression on her face, almost as if she was surprised by the kindness.

"I'll check back with you later," the older woman said as she took out the pencil she'd stuck behind her ear and then moved to the next table.

Liza reached for her second cherry, while eyeing the pretzels. "I wonder if the gang still goes to Latitude Thirty-Three," she said with an unexpected wistfulness.

"I think they do. If you want we can go there after—"

"God, no." She took a quick sip of her drink. "No one from *Just Between Us* wants to see me."

"Why were you in the parking lot yesterday?"

She frowned. "Can we talk about something else?"

"Name it. I can't seem to get it right."

She tilted her head to the side, her eyebrows drawing together. "I don't get you."

"Me? I'm an open book."

"Are you married?"

That annoyed him. "I wouldn't be sitting here if I were."

Liza shrugged. "Why? This is merely a friendly drink, yes? Plus, you're celibate."

He smiled. "I was ten minutes ago."

She shook her head in mock exasperation. "Okay, were you ever married?"

"No."

"Hmm."

"What does that mean?"

"You seem like the marrying kind. Kids. The white picket fence. Steady. Stable. You know the type."

Evan knew exactly what she meant. Liza was on the wild side, which meant she'd find someone like that boring. The thing was, he pretty much was that guy. He would have had it all by now if Angela hadn't screwed him. And, literally, two of his friends. "I have the white picket fence. Came with the house."

Liza chuckled. "Ah, so you do have the whole house-and-mortgage thing."

"Gotta live somewhere."

Her expression fell and her shoulders sagged. "I think I'd like a house someday," she said softly. "With a small yard and garden. Apartment living is getting old."

"Where are you now?"

She looked warily at him. "You wouldn't know the place. Anyway, I'm not even sure I'm staying in Atlanta. Probably won't. Too hot and humid."

"Great for growing gardens."

She gave a shrug of indifference and in just those few seconds she became the old Liza. "I'm not really the hearth-and-home type. I was only making conversation."

"Ah, I see." He didn't really. Better to let it go, though. "You must have something in mind, assuming you win the lawsuit."

She'd just picked up her drink and it slid from her hand. Half the liquid sloshed onto her lap before she could right the glass. "Damn."

He rose. "I'll get a towel from the waitress."

"No, that's okay. I've got it." She used both their cocktail napkins but he knew that couldn't have done much good.

"I can get a towel."

"No," she said curtly, and then took a furtive look around before staring back down at her lap.

Only the couple at the next table had noticed, and they'd already restarted their conversation.

Evan just watched her swipe at her jeans with an angry frustration that went well beyond a spilled drink. She bit her lower lip so hard he wouldn't be surprised if she drew blood. He wanted to help, to at least say something comforting or funny to distract her, but he knew better. He had this really strong and unexpected feeling that Liza needed to battle her own demons.

THIS WAS SO STUPID. She wasn't about to dry her jeans this way, but she didn't want to meet Evan's eyes. Bet he was sorry that he'd asked her out. Served him right. What had he expected?

"Excuse me," she said finally. "I need to go to the restroom and take care of this."

She only briefly looked at him as she slid out of

her seat. There was no pity in his eyes, not even curiosity. In fact, she didn't know what to make of his bland expression.

"Shall I order you another drink?" he asked calmly.

"No, thanks," she murmured, and gave him her back as she blindly searched for the ladies' room.

It had to be in one of the corners, and it was the second place she looked. She didn't give a damn about her jeans and went straight to the sink. She turned on the faucet and splashed her face with cold water. At the last moment she remembered that she'd actually applied a little makeup before coming out. Too late now.

Didn't matter, though. Unlikely she'd see Evan again. He probably couldn't wait to finish his drink and get rid of her. She wouldn't be surprised if he'd already paid the bill. Ironically, she'd enjoyed being with him. He wasn't as stuffy as she'd expected him to be. Still not her type, but he'd been pleasant company. Didn't take her crap, either. Always a refreshing discovery.

The problem was, she hadn't found out anything about the lawsuit. She knew damn well people gossiped around there, especially in the coffee room. Evan wasn't the type to participate, but he still might've heard something useful.

Staring at her reflection in the mirror, she cringed at the dark circles under her eyes. A couple of years away from the big 3-0 and she already had pronounced crow's-feet at the corners of her eyes. Her skin was too pale, and now that she'd washed off the tinted moisturizer, she really looked like hell.

She pushed the hair away from her face and, as she'd seen her mother do a hundred times, a zillion years ago, Liza pinched her cheeks to give them some color. She didn't do a very good job because the right side looked more like a bad mosquito bite. Great.

She grabbed a couple of paper towels and blotted her jeans, and then washed the stickiness off her hands. If Evan hadn't already bolted, she'd come right out and ask him what he'd heard about the lawsuit. All he could do was tell her to get lost. But she doubted he'd do that. He was too much of a gentleman. And damn it, she liked that.

3

LIZA'S HEART DID A funny little hop as she approached the table, and he smiled. His hair was too short for her taste, but he had great eyes, the perfect shade of whiskey-brown, and a square jaw with a dimple in the center of his chin that she found terribly appealing. That he had some stubble and wasn't clean-shaven, as usual, was right up her alley.

The table had been cleaned off and her empty glass had been replaced with another tequila sunrise. She reclaimed her seat and noticed that he was also on his second beer. Guess he wasn't going to run screaming from the room.

"Trust me with another drink, I see." She decided not to point out that she'd said she didn't want another.

"I asked for a lid but they didn't have one."

She smiled in spite of herself. Either she was really starved for male company or Evan was truly turning out to be less stodgy than she'd perceived him.

"What kind of doctor are you?" she asked, genuinely interested.

"An internist."

"How did you get the consulting gig for *Heartbeat?*"

"The producer is an old frat brother of mine."

"From med school?"

He chuckled. "Undergraduate. You don't have time for a fraternity in med school. Between working and studying I was lucky to get four hours of sleep a night."

"Here I thought you were one of those rich kids who had a trust fund."

"Yeah, right."

"Seriously, I did. You seem the preppy type."

"Bad assumption. I just finally paid off my student loans, thanks to the consulting job."

"I still have ten thousand outstanding myself." Liza had no idea why she'd offered the information. It galled her to know that part of her inheritance had been used to buy Rick's bike instead of making her debt-free.

"That's not bad."

"I guess not. Though I don't like to owe any money."

"Me, too. My parents scraped together every penny to pay down their mortgage. The day they made their last payment they had a huge barbecue in the backyard and invited all the relatives and neighbors."

Liza smiled at the fondness in his voice. "You have a big family?"

"Two brothers. Lots of cousins, most of whom live here in Atlanta. How about you?"

"No siblings. Except Eve and Jane. They're like—" She cut herself off, horrified at what she'd revealed. It was Evan's fault. He was just too damn easy to talk to.

He looked clearly curious, but graciously filled the conversation gap. "My father is retiring in three months. He and Mom are thinking about buying a small condo in Florida but they're not sure where. You're from Jacksonville, aren't you?"

"I was a kid when I lived there, and then I left after college." She quickly picked up her drink and took a cooling sip. She didn't like this warm squishy feeling of gratitude. Evan didn't need information on Florida. He could've asked her all kinds of awkward questions. Not that she'd have answered, but still.

"Are your parents living there—in Jacksonville?"

"My dad died last year. My mom is there."

She didn't know where exactly, but that wasn't something she'd share. Besides, with his background, he wouldn't understand what it was like growing up with an alcoholic and a pill-popper.

"I'm sorry about your father."

"Yeah. Guess it was his time." She looked away so she wouldn't see the revulsion on Evan's face. She hadn't meant to sound so callous, but a life of hard drinking never ended well. When she finally looked at Evan again, he smiled kindly. It annoyed her. Why was he so nice? What the hell did he want from her? She didn't deserve his kindness. Or anyone else's. Didn't he understand that?

"You getting hungry?"

"Why?"

"Well," he said slowly, the corners of his mouth twitching, "it's approaching the dinner hour and traditionally people eat a meal at that time."

"I'm not traditional."

"True." He loosened the knot on his tie. "That's what I like about you."

"Hmm." She couldn't come up with anything witty to say. She was too busy watching his long fingers work, and noticing the smattering of hair across the back of his hands. His skin was tan and more rugged-looking than she'd expect of a doctor. Probably belonged to a golf or tennis club.

"Liza?"

"What?"

He frowned at her. "I asked if you'd like to go to dinner."

"Dinner?"

"Uh-huh, you know, eating."

She glanced at her watch, shocked at how much time had passed. Yet she hadn't gotten a word out of him about the scuttlebutt around the station. Rick had been sleeping when she left, and she wanted him to stay that way until she was safely in her apartment. "I can't. I'm leaving after this drink."

"All right." He looked disappointed as he leaned back in his chair. His shoulders really were quite broad. She wondered what he'd be like without the jacket. "Another time, maybe?"

She nodded absently. He kind of looked like a jock. Not her favorite. But he definitely seemed as if he were in shape. The most exercise she got these days was climbing the stairs to her apartment.

"Your enthusiasm is heartening."

"What?"

He smiled sadly. "One of the other things I like about you is your directness. If you don't want a repeat, go ahead and say so. You're not going to hurt my feelings."

"That's not it." She cleared her throat. What a great opening he'd handed her. "It's this whole lawsuit thing making me crazy. I'm not myself."

"Ah. I understand."

She fingered her straw, keeping her gaze lowered, hoping she sounded casual. "Have you heard anything?"

"About what?"

"The lawsuit. My attorney thinks they're about to make another offer."

"Good." He slowly set down his beer, clearly avoiding her gaze. "I'm sure everyone wants to put this behind them."

"But you haven't heard anything?"

This time he looked her straight in the eye. "Is that why you called? So you could pump me for information?"

"Yes."

He didn't even blink at her bluntness. "Sorry you wasted your time." His expression grim, he reached into his pocket. "And mine."

"Wait. Initially I did want to meet with you so that I could find out what was going on."

He pulled out some bills from his silver-and-turquoise money clip and picked up the check the waitress had left.

Liza plucked the slip of paper out of his hand. "I called you. I'm paying."

"Will that assuage your guilt?"

"Had you been listening, you'd realize that I qualified my answer. This evening turned out to be a pleasant surprise."

His mouth curved in a patronizing smile.

"Look, I'm glad I came, okay?" She dug through her purse, searching for her wallet. Mostly, she didn't want to face Evan. Screw him. At least she'd told him the truth. She could've gone all dewy-eyed and saccharine-sweet to get what she wanted. But she hadn't. Not that she'd ever use that tactic in a million years.

"Liza?"

Grudgingly, she looked up at him.

His gentle smile disarmed her. "I'm glad you came, too."

"Yeah, well, now that the mutual admiration society has met, time to get out of here." She found a twenty and looked at the bill. God. Even the beer was expensive in this place. She started fishing in her wallet again, but Evan reached over and touched her hand.

"I'm getting this," he said and before she knew it, he grabbed the check out of her fingers.

"Give me that."

"Nope." He already had the money ready and handed the bills to the waitress as she passed by on her way to another table.

"This is the twenty-first century, in case you've just woken up."

"A gentleman supersedes any period in time."

"Oh, brother."

"You ready?"

"You can stay."

He snorted. "Right."

"So now you're insisting on walking me to my car?"

"You bet."

She shook her head as they both got to their feet. "You're something else."

Winking at her, he took her arm with a flourish, the way his grandfather might have escorted his wife.

Liza laughed. "What am I going to do with you?"

His smile was far from patronizing when he asked, "Open to suggestions?"

As THEY LEFT THE BAR, Evan placed his hand at the small of her back. She was pretty thin, which revived his earlier suspicion regarding her health. Yet her coloring was good and her energy level didn't seem to be lacking.

"You've lost some weight," he said once they got on the sidewalk and he'd positioned himself on the outside. Rush-hour traffic hadn't subsided, and it wouldn't for another couple of hours.

She frowned slightly. "Have I?"

"Must be the stress of the lawsuit."

She moved away, self-consciously wrapping her arms around herself. "I guess."

"You want my jacket?"

"Huh? Oh, no. Thanks."

"By the way, I haven't heard anything about the lawsuit."

She turned back to him, lowering her arms, suddenly interested again. "Nothing?"

"Nada." He shook his head. "But I'm not in the loop around the station. When I'm done for the day, I'm out of there."

She turned away again, clearly disappointed.

"Sorry."

"It's okay."

Was it? Now that she knew he couldn't be of use to her, would she still go out with him again? "I wish you luck, though."

She slowed. "Do you? Why?"

"Because you apparently believe you have a claim. I don't know the particulars, but—"

"Don't give me that. The story's been splashed across the damn newspaper."

"Do you believe everything you read?" he shot back and enjoyed the bewilderment on her face.

She stared at him for a long moment and then picked up the pace again, her eyebrows pinched together in a fierce frown. "I don't understand you," she muttered.

"I believe you've already pointed that out." He

tried not to smile and show just how much he enjoyed puzzling her. She was a bit of a wild one, and he absolutely wasn't. But that didn't mean he didn't like a taste of the exotic once in a while.

"Yes, well, things haven't changed."

Evan finally smiled. "How about tomorrow night?"

"What about it?"

"Dinner, and a chance to figure me out."

Her lips started to turn up, and then she sighed and shook her head. "I can't."

"Okay, how about Thursday night?"

"I can't."

"In other words, I should quit asking." He watched her closely, hoping he was wrong. Hoping that she hadn't merely been using him tonight.

She looked down at her hands and pressed her lips together. "I surprisingly had fun tonight…."

"Thanks," he said dryly.

"I'm awful. I know. But that's the truth. I expected you to be different," she said, reminding him how much he found her frankness refreshing.

"Somehow I sense a 'but' coming."

"I can't see you again."

"Okay," he said slowly, realizing he deserved the mental slap. "Seeing someone else?"

"No," she said quickly.

Annoyed with himself, he kept walking beside her, facing straight ahead. He shouldn't have asked if there was another guy in the picture. The lady said no. That was enough. He was raised better than that.

They continued in silence to the station's parking lot. Along the street, Christmas decorations were everywhere. Lights were strung around telephone poles and animated Santas and reindeers blinked from merchants' windows. It was enough to sour his sudden precarious mood.

Damn, but he wished his parents would go to Florida for the holidays. But, no, they insisted on staying so the family could have a festive dinner together. They probably only maintained the tradition to keep Evan's spirits up.

Ironically, getting together or even acknowledging the holidays was the last thing he wanted to do. Better to hide out at home, play some tunes, read a good book. And try not to think about Angela. About how this Christmas Eve would've been their seventh anniversary.

"Well, we're here."

He snapped out of his reverie. They'd already gotten to his brand-new Camry, and Liza was staring at him with open wonder.

"Thank you, Evan. I had a great time. Really."

He motioned for her to keep walking. She started to protest and then closed her lush, pink mouth when she must have realized that he was going to walk her to her car whether she liked it or not.

Most of the lot was unusually empty for this time of day. Then he remembered hearing that one of the departments was having a Christmas party tonight. Otherwise, no one left until the director had his or her perfect shot. He saw Liza's compact about a half dozen stalls away. The car was an older model and didn't come with the convenience of a remote so he waited until she manually unlocked her door.

She got it open and then stood back. "I wish you would've let me pay the check."

He smiled. "You're welcome."

She made a face. "I'm getting in now so you can leave knowing you've done your gentlemanly duty."

He held the door for her until she was sitting behind the wheel. It took a good deal of willpower not to lean over and kiss her. Just a brief touching of lips. Nothing threatening. But she probably wouldn't welcome the overture and he wasn't one to push. "Drive safely," he said, and closed the door.

Before he could walk away, she promptly rolled down the window. A floodlight from the building shined on her face, making her hazel eyes glitter. "I really did have a nice time, Evan."

"Who are you trying to convince?"

She smiled. "Okay, I deserved that."

"For the record, me, too," he said and headed for his car before he gave in to his impulse and did something foolish. The woman wasn't interested. He was a mature adult. He could accept that he wasn't her type. Didn't have to like it, but he could certainly accept the fact.

He got out his keys and used the remote to unlock the car doors. He was too busy to be dating, anyway. As it was, his receptionist constantly begged him to expand his office hours. She was tired of turning away patients. In about three years he figured he could quit consulting on the television show and start looking toward the future. Build a nice solid practice, work hard, retire early if he chose. Although he doubted it, because he really did like practicing medicine. The consulting job was a necessity for now.

He took off his jacket and laid it across the backseat before slipping in behind the wheel. It was cool for a moment, but then he turned the key in the ignition and both the promise of warmth and soft rock filled the air. The radio was too loud, but the volume always was deafening when he first started the car. Funny how it never seemed loud when he parked. Maybe that's why he never remembered to adjust it.

The sun had recently set, leaving a pink tinge along the horizon, but it was dark enough that he glanced in his rearview mirror to make sure Liza had safely left the parking lot. Her car was still there. He squinted but he couldn't see her behind the wheel. What the hell...

He grabbed the handle and jerked open the car door. He got out, and she was right there, so close, he nearly knocked her over.

"Liza, what's wrong?" He gripped her upper arms.

"I'm okay," she said with a nervous laugh. "Really, I'm okay."

He didn't let go of her. It felt good being this close. Close enough to feel her warm breath brush his chin. Close enough to smell the vanilla scent that clung to her hair.

"Evan? You're kind of hurting my arm."

"Oh, jeez." He quickly lowered his hands. "I'm sorry." He gave her some room. "What happened? Is something wrong with your car?"

"No, no. My car is fine." She briefly glanced over her shoulder. "Well, other than it looks as if it's been through a war zone. Can I change my mind about tomorrow night?"

That took him aback. "Sure."

"Ever been to Simone's?"

He smiled. No problem. She could choose the restaurant. "No, but I know of it."

"How about seven?"

"That works for me."

"Good." She hesitated, and then took a small step back. "Thanks again for tonight."

"My pleasure." Was it his imagination or was she reluctant to leave? "I'll wait until you start your car."

She sighed. "Good night, then."

"Good night."

She made a sound of exasperation and came toward him. He was only about five inches taller, but she grabbed a fistful of his shirt and pulled him down to her mouth.

She hesitated, as if she'd changed her mind. He smelled her fear, and gently coaxed her lips to soften. Then they parted slightly and he readily accepted the invitation, slipping his tongue inside and exploring the tempting fleshy part of the inside of her cheek. She responded briefly. When she pulled back, he didn't push. That was enough. For now.

4

"DON'T WALK AWAY FROM ME, you stupid bitch."

Liza foolishly hesitated before continuing toward the apartment door. The next second, she felt Rick's vile hand grip her shoulder. He jerked her so hard she spun around. That was the second time he'd actually touched her in anger.

She took a deep breath and in a low voice said, "Don't ever do that again."

"Or what?" His blue eyes were bloodshot, and the long blond hair she used to find so hot was tangled and matted after not seeing a comb for a week.

"Or I'll withdraw the lawsuit and you can find another meal ticket."

He laughed uproariously. "Bullshit. We both know you won't do that."

"Don't be so damn sure." She was so tired of him—the lifestyle, the lies—and she had a feeling he saw it in her face because for the first time, she saw fear in his.

"Come on, Liza." He went to put his arm around her but she ducked away.

"I mean it, Rick. I don't want you touching me."

She looked at the dirty clothes piling up on the floor in the corner of the living room. Empty booze bottles and beer cans vied for space with crumpled fast-food wrappers on all available tabletops. She didn't even want to know what had created the brown stains in the beige carpet.

Careful not to make contact, he stuck a finger in her face. "Better watch your friggin' mouth. Looks like you're forgetting who has the diaries."

She stepped back. Not because she was afraid, but because he smelled so bad. He'd been wearing the same ripped blue T-shirt two days ago and she seriously doubted it had been washed since then. Or whether he'd had a shower in the past week.

Most disgusting of all was the fact that she'd ever found him attractive. A little over a year ago she'd been so damn in love with him that she would've done anything to keep him. How pathetically certain she'd been that he was the one. The one man who could make her whole. Heal all the scars from childhood. Show her the love her parents had been incapable of giving. Sure, he'd been attentive and charming at first. Sexy and somewhat dangerous. Turned out he was just another boozing addict like them. How could she have been so blind and stupid?

"Look," she said finally, "we're taking the next offer they present."

"Is that what that jackass attorney is telling you?" Rick threw the beer he'd had in his hand across the room. "You think I can live on half a million?"

With all that stuff he was shooting in his arm, he

probably couldn't. His problem, not hers. "I haven't even talked to the attorney. This is my decision. I can't live like this anymore."

"What do you mean you haven't talked to the attorney?"

Too late. She remembered that's where she'd told him she was going when she met Evan yesterday. "I got the date of our appointment mixed up."

His gaze narrowed in suspicion. "You banging him?" The telltale tic started at the side of his throat. He was going to start losing it. "You better not be banging him."

"Grow up. I want him to get the money so I can get you off my back." Again, she headed for the door. He wouldn't stop her this time. He needed a fix. "And you damn well better have the diaries for me before I hand over a dime."

A few seconds after she closed the door behind her, she heard something hit it. She hurried toward her apartment, comforted by the knowledge that he'd pass out soon. Truth be told, she was becoming afraid of him. He was getting more agitated and his appetite for heroine more voracious. She just hoped his brain didn't get too fried before he turned over Eve's diaries.

Next time she had to give him money she was slipping it under the door. No more stepping a single foot in his apartment. And if he made a scene outside of hers, she'd threaten to call the police. She was pretty certain that would keep him away without jeopardizing exposure of the diaries.

As soon as she locked her own door, she went straight to the bedroom and sprawled out on the unmade bed. She would have to start getting ready for dinner in an hour. But a quick nap would really help. By the time she had to go, Rick would be out of it and she wouldn't have to worry about him chasing her to the parking lot like he'd done last week when she'd simply planned on going to the market.

She pulled the covers over her body and closed her eyes. Ten minutes later sleep hadn't come. Not unusual. Sleep was a luxury these days. Something else Rick had stolen from her. When she'd worked as a producer for *Just Between Us* there had been many long stressful days. But none of them compared to what she'd experienced in the past year.

If she wasn't lying awake worrying that Eve's diaries would somehow make it to the tabloids, Liza would be stressing over how she was going to make the rest of the money stretch out until the lawsuit was settled. If she didn't get awarded anything, that would bring on a whole new set of problems. Rick would blame her, of course.

She had no idea what she'd do then. Other than going to Eve and Jane and explain why she needed the money from the lawsuit. It was also the very last thing she wanted to do. Admitting that she'd deliberately gone against Eve's wishes and taken Rick to help pack up Grammie's house after she'd died was the least of it. The diaries Rick has stolen had spanned some troubled years for Eve.

Her parents had tragically died in a car accident and Eve's charmed life had ended at age eleven, although she'd been taken in by her wonderful, loving grandmother, and in a way Grammie had taken Liza in, too. Home had been such a horrific place for Liza, and Grammie's house had been a refuge. She even cooked. Real meals. Not mushy frozen stuff. And the stories she would tell. Wonderful, colorful stories that were so real Liza would dream about them at night.

Even after she and Eve and Jane had gone off to college, it was Grammie's house where they congregated for holidays. The news of her sudden death had been like a dagger to Liza's heart. Her own father's death hadn't hit her nearly as hard. Not even close. That was her only excuse for taking Rick that weekend to Grammie's. Eve had been so devastated that she was incapable of packing up the old house. She'd asked Liza, who, devastated herself by the woman's passing, felt she needed Rick's support to complete the task.

God, how incredibly dumb she'd been.

She dragged the covers over her head. Eve had always been the best of friends, and Liza betrayed her. Life had been hell since then. Justice was definitely being served.

No, if justice was truly being doled out, she wouldn't have run across Evan again. She smiled, thinking about how he'd insisted on walking on the outside of the sidewalk. Such a goof. And that kiss. Holy crap. Who knew the guy could kiss like that?

Plus, she'd had a really nice evening. At times she'd even forgotten her mission to find out about the lawsuit. But then, it was a long shot that he'd be privy to any information.

Damn, she was anxious to see him again. Disturbing thought, really. He totally wasn't her type. The timing was definitely wrong. Nothing to fret over. It was the nonthreatening adult conversation that appealed to her, especially when that aspect of her life was woefully lacking.

During the past few minutes, she'd gotten drowsy. Thinking about Evan. Smiling, she rolled over and buried her face in the pillow. He'd be real happy when she pointed out to him that he'd put her to sleep.

EVAN DIDN'T HAVE TO check his watch again to know he'd been stood up. Damn her. She could've found a way to get a hold of him instead of letting him sit here for forty-five minutes drinking by himself. Ironically, he'd thought about giving her his cell phone number in case she had to cancel, but he hadn't wanted to make it that easy for her to back out.

Apparently he was wrong about her. She was an assertive woman and sometimes others felt threatened by that quality. Clearly, she really could be that self-absorbed. That's okay. Now he knew. He was done with her.

He downed the rest of his wine and looked around for the waitress. The place was small, holding only ten tables, but he didn't see her. He supposed he could go ahead and eat. The menu was okay. Traditional items, mostly. Certainly reasonable. The décor was nothing to speak of, with mass-produced photos of different kinds of flowers on the light-green walls. The tables were covered with white tablecloths, and each one had a fresh flower in a vase.

If the place had been busy, he would've been out of here by now. But besides him, only three other tables were occupied. Obviously not a popular restaurant. And definitely not one he would have expected Liza to have chosen.

He heard the front door open. He would've had a clear view of anyone who entered if not for the coatrack. Not that he thought she'd finally decided to grace him with her presence. He knew at least half a dozen women who'd accept his offer of a date before he got the last word out. Not because he was good-looking or well-built or anything other he had a degree from Harvard medical school.

That didn't impress Liza. In fact, he had a feeling that for her it was a deterrent. Maybe her indifference was what he found appealing. Or maybe because she was the exact opposite of Angela.

Liza came into view and everything else faded.

Her long hair had that slightly wild look he liked so much. Not on most women, but Liza pulled it off. The short denim skirt showed off her long shapely legs, but another bulky sweater, this one black, hid everything else. Again, she wasn't wearing a coat.

He should be angry but he was too glad to see her. After she sat down across from him he said, "I'd just given up on you. I was ready to leave."

"I'm so, so sorry. I took a nap and overslept."

"You could have called. I'm listed and my service would have gotten the message to me."

"I know." She fidgeted with her napkin. "But if I called, I might have chickened out and canceled."

"Now why would you do that?"

She wore only the barest hint of makeup, but enough to bring out the green flecks in her hazel eyes. "There's a limit even to my bluntness," she said, glancing around at the people at the other tables. She seemed a little edgy.

"You look great."

Her tongue darted out to moisten her peach-colored lips. "Thank you," she said softly, shifting as if uncomfortable with the compliment and picking up the menu the waitress had left for her. "Have you looked at this?"

"About seven times."

She glanced up at him. "I was rude, I apologized, if you can't get past that, then—"

"Take it easy. I'm only teasing."

"Sorry. I don't wake up well."

A crash came from the kitchen and Liza just about flew out of her seat. She put a hand to her throat. "Scared the hell out of me."

"I noticed." He sensed there was something

more than the loud noise making her jumpy. "This place a favorite of yours?"

She glanced around with a slight frown. "Actually, this is my first time here."

"I didn't think this seemed like your style."

"No?"

"Is it?"

"Tell me how you arrived at your diagnosis, Dr. Gann."

"A premed student would've come to the same conclusion. This place is too tame. Too ordinary."

"Really." She tossed her hair back over her shoulder and leaned forward. "Describe the kind of place you think I'd like."

He put his elbows on the table and met her halfway. "How about I show you instead?"

Her gaze slowly moved down to his mouth, then went to his chin and lingered. "I'm listening."

"No more talking. I lead, you follow. You have to trust me."

"And if I don't?"

Shrugging, he leaned back. "Your loss."

The waitress showed up to take her order, and Liza looked hesitantly at him.

"Your call," he said.

"Thanks, but I won't be having a drink."

The waitress readied her pad. "Ready to order dinner then?"

"We won't be having dinner after all. I'll take the check when you have a moment," Evan said, aware of the flash of dismay on the woman's face.

Still, she smiled pleasantly as she dug into the pocket of her white apron, produced the check for his glass of chardonnay and laid it down on the table.

He got out his silver money clip. The one Angela had given him for his twenty-sixth birthday and the only memento of her he kept. The perfect reminder to keep him from being stupid about a woman again.

"No rush on that," the waitress said. "You folks have a nice evening."

"You, too." He'd missed Atlanta while he was away at school. The city had grown dramatically since he was a kid but there was still a basic niceness that hadn't disappeared. The woman had to be disappointed that she wasn't going to rack up a hefty tip, but she remained gracious.

Evan included an extra twenty and laid the money and check facedown. He pushed back his chair. "Ready?"

Liza got up and walked alongside him to the door. He stopped to get his coat and noticed her peering intently out of the window into the darkness.

"Anything wrong?"

She turned to him abruptly. "No. Why?"

He shrugged into the camel-colored cashmere coat he'd found at an end-of-season sale last year. Still, it seemed like a big splurge when he'd had so many student loans. "I don't know. I thought maybe someone was stealing your car."

She adjusted his collar with a familiarity that

startled him. "Then they'd be doing me a huge favor." Their eyes met and she quickly lowered her hands.

"I don't suppose you have a coat with you," he said and continued buttoning.

"What do you think?"

"Right." He opened the door and she preceded him into the dark parking lot. "My car okay?"

"I could follow you."

"Promise to have you back anytime you say."

She looked tentative at first, but then nodded and followed him to the Camry. She smiled when he opened the passenger door for her. He did it out of habit, but was rewarded when she swung her long legs into the car and her skirt rode up to an indecent height. She saw him watching and he immediately closed the door.

The air was cool and damp, which could easily ruin his plans. Although he did have a blanket in his trunk that would help. He got behind the wheel and immediately turned on the engine. Fortunately, the heater did its job. Liza had to be chilled, no matter what she said.

He heard the passenger window go down and turned to her in astonishment. She slid her finger over the control and it went back up.

She looked over at him. "Wow. A grown-up car. Real automatic windows and everything."

"I even have an automatic hood. Want to play with it?"

"May I?"

Evan smiled as he pulled into traffic. "You win that lawsuit and you can have any kind of car you want."

Her grin disappeared and she turned to stare out of the window.

"I say something wrong?"

"I'm not doing it for the money," she said quietly.

"Your business." He hadn't been prying. He hadn't even given thought to his words. They'd just come out.

After a long silence she asked, "Where are we going, anyway?"

"You like Chinese?"

"I like the noodles and sweet-and-sour chicken."

"Good."

"So where—"

"You're not allowed any more questions."

She snorted. "Says who?"

It was a moot question since they'd reached their destination. He pulled into a spot in front of the small mom-and-pop take-out place and turned off the engine. There was a short counter where customers occasionally ate, but primarily it was a to-go business with three different entrée choices each day. Fortunately, vegetable chow mein and sweet-and-sour chicken were a staple.

"You coming?" he asked after he'd opened his door and she was still sitting there.

"I have to make a phone call. It's kind of important." She averted her eyes. "And private."

Evan stared back. Hell, yeah, he minded. He wouldn't if she hadn't looked so guilty. What the devil was going on? Was this Angela all over again?

LIZA COULD TELL he was angry. He had every right. Through the glass window she watched him order their food while she listened to the fifth ring. Next it would go to voice mail. And then she could relax.

Just as she'd hoped, she heard the switch-over to the computer voice that gave instructions to leave a message. Liza flipped the phone closed, and breathed a sigh of relief. It meant Rick wouldn't be bothering her tonight.

All she needed was for him to be lurking in the shadows and have followed her to Evan's, assuming that's what he had in mind. She couldn't imagine where else they'd be going to eat takeout. It was probably her imagination but she could've sworn someone had been on her tail ever since she left the apartment complex. More than likely it was her strained nerves after the fight she'd had with Rick that had made her late.

That he was actually on his feet and semicoherent had caught her totally off guard. With the amount of booze and heroin that she assumed he had in his system, he should have been flat on his face. Instead, he was staggering around, although he probably wouldn't remember a thing tomorrow.

Still, she couldn't help looking over her shoulder. For the first time today she'd stood up to him. Actually threatened him, and possibly made the grave mistake of driving him to desperation. Best thing she could do from now until the settlement was to stay away. Give him money when he asked. Whether it was for drugs or booze or food, she didn't give a damn.

She laid her head back against the leather seat and continued to watch Evan. He really was a nice guy. Even though he wasn't her type, spending time with him had reminded her of what it had been like to have a real life. To simply enjoy a stress-free dinner out with a friend, and not have to constantly check the time as if she were a sixteen-year-old with a curfew.

It didn't take him long to come out carrying a large white bag. He opened the door and handed it to her without saying a word. If she wanted to salvage the evening, she had to apologize. She just wasn't sure how, without doling out too much information or start crying on his shoulder. Yeah, like that would happen.

"Smells good," she finally said after they'd gotten back on the road.

He nodded. Didn't even spare her a glance.

She took a deep breath. It didn't help. "Look, if you wanted cookies and milk, you should've called your mother for a date."

He looked over at her then, as if she'd totally gone out of her mind. "You are really something. You know that?"

"'Something' not being good, I take it."

"To tell you the truth…" He pushed a frustrated hand through his short hair. "I don't know."

Liza grinned. "Okay, so I have a fifty-fifty chance. I'll take it."

He shook his head, pretending disgust, but she saw the corners of his mouth twitch.

Satisfied, she sat back in the comfy leather seat, and thought about that kiss.

5

THEY WEREN'T ON THE ROAD long when Evan turned
off. Or maybe it was because he'd been quiet and
she'd been daydreaming that the time seemed to go
by so fast, but they definitely weren't in a residen-
tial area. "Where are we?"

"A park."

"I can see that."

He took the bag from her. "You want to eat in
here or outside?"

She looked around, not that she could see much,
except for a picnic bench not too far away from the
car. Half of the trees were bare, the other half were
huge pines that kept the place from looking too
stark. The lighting was poor except in the parking
lot. Normal people didn't wander around in forty-
degree weather.

"I have a blanket in the trunk, but it's your call."

She grinned at him. "You devil."

"The blanket is part of an emergency kit," he
said dryly. "I keep it in the car at all times."

"Of course," she said just as dryly. How could
she have thought otherwise? In fact, he hadn't

even tried to take her to his house, like she'd expected.

After last night's kiss, she thought perhaps Dudley Do-Right might have a wild streak in him. Might even ignore the gentleman's dating rule book he probably kept on his nightstand. A kiss on the cheek after the second date. The lips came after the third date, but only briefly. By the eighth date he might even get bold and try to cop a feel.

Not that they would have that many dates, so if she wanted to get laid she'd have to make the first move.

The thought of seducing and shocking him cheered her immeasurably. "Outside," she said finally. "We can share the blanket."

"You got it."

He left the bag and got out of the car to go around to the trunk. She waited until she could see him from the side mirror, the blanket draped over his arm, then grabbed the bag of food and got out to meet him.

They walked toward the picnic bench together, and she had to admit, she was pretty cold. Her legs, mostly, because of the short skirt. She'd be damned if she'd admit it, though, after all that bluster over not needing a coat. She shivered. Maybe they should've stayed in the car.

He didn't say a word, just placed the folded blanket over her shoulders and adjusted it so that it protected her bare neck. She didn't object. She kind of liked the way he fussed over her. It was different. Nice. Sort of sweet.

The uneven sidewalk, combined with the darkness and the odd pinecone underfoot, made it difficult to walk, but he kept his hand cupped over her elbow and she had no doubt that he wouldn't let her fall.

They got to the table, and between the trees she got a glimpse of a stream of gold and red city lights angled below them. "Wow!"

"Nice, huh?"

"Who knew?" The area he'd chosen was slightly elevated and if they were fool enough to venture farther there would undoubtedly be a great view. "I'm not sure where we are."

"A secret place."

Grinning, she set down the plastic bag. Two more minutes and the food was going to be cold. She didn't care. She watched him wipe off the bench for her, making sure it was dry and free of leaves and pebbles before he gestured for her to sit.

"If it gets too cold at anytime, we'll go back to the car, okay?"

She nodded. "I thought you were taking me to your house."

He smiled. "I thought about it."

"But?"

"I didn't want you to misunderstand."

"Misunderstand what?"

His low chuckle made her want to see his expression. But the light was behind him, which meant he could see her but she couldn't see him. No fair.

"After all, you are a guy," she said, and felt a

surge of heat when he slid in next to her, his thigh warming hers, his elbow brushing the side of her breast.

"Last time I looked." He pulled out a white carton and a pair of chopsticks. "Here."

"I don't know how to use those things. I've tried, but it isn't pretty."

"Then you'll need these," he said and set a stack of white paper napkins in front of her. "Don't let them blow away. I don't want to be running around in the dark trying to pick them up."

She didn't doubt he'd do just that. Every last napkin would be accounted for before he'd leave. She hated litter herself, but she wasn't anal about it.

She looked in the bag in case he was kidding. No plastic utensils. "You're implying I should use my fingers."

"If you're hungry enough."

"I guess I can spear with the best of them."

"Look, it's easy to use chopsticks. I'll show you." He slid an arm around her and pulled her against his chest, close enough to run his arms along hers until his hand covered her hand. "Pick up the chopsticks."

Silly the way her heart slammed inside her chest. Made getting a grip on the stupid bamboo sticks really, really hard. Her fingers shook and she dropped the utensils once before securing them firmly in her hand.

"Okay?"

"Ready," she said.

"Rest one stick against the length of your middle finger like this." He maneuvered her fingers so that she had it aligned with the chopstick. "The other one you hold between your thumb and forefinger."

She tried to do as he said, and the sticks flew into the air. One landed on the table and stayed, the other one rolled off the side onto the ground.

"I'll get it." He withdrew his arm from around her to look under the table.

In the next second, she felt his warm breath on her bare thigh. His roughened chin scraped the skin at the side of her left knee. Instinctively she wanted to squeeze her legs together, but she resisted and tried to breathe in deeply. It wasn't as if he was going to do anything down there. Not that she'd mind if he did do a little exploring.

He came up too quickly. Clearing his throat, he tossed the recovered chopstick into the empty bag. "Good thing I picked up a spare pair."

"Of course you did." She noticed he hadn't looked at her. Was he embarrassed?

"What does that mean?"

"You're like a Boy Scout. Always prepared."

The light caught his wicked smile. "And that's a problem how…?"

A light, chilly breeze had her pulling the blanket tighter around her shoulders. "Now that I think about it—"

Evan's mouth came down hard on hers. She hadn't expected it and the blanket slipped from her fingers. She didn't need it anymore. Heat traveled all the way down to her toes. She could hardly breathe.

She didn't care. His practiced tongue dove deep and probed every recess of her mouth, using just the right amount of pressure and speed to taunt her, to make her crave more. He framed her face with his hands, and she gripped his shoulders. It wasn't easy twisting around like that to face him and her skirt hem rose nearly to her panties.

She really wanted him to slide his hand along her bare skin. Usually she wasn't shy about making known what she wanted, but she wasn't sure with Evan. This would be a hell of a time to scare him off. But then again, he did start it all.

He eased up and pulled back a little, but she wasn't ready to quit. She didn't want to upset the rhythm. She leaned in to him and he lowered one hand, his palm skimming the outside of her arm, dipping at her waist and then molding against her hip. He finally rested his hand on her thigh. He traced a finger to her panties and then stopped, pulling all the way back so that he could look at her.

"You have to be freezing."

"Not so much."

"What happened to the blanket?" He reached behind her and apparently saw that half of it had fallen to the ground.

"Don't worry about it."

"But I—"

She grabbed hold of his shirt, pulled him close and whispered, "For once, don't be a gentleman."

A flash of white teeth and then he claimed her mouth again. No sweet start. No gentle brush of the lips. He plunged his tongue inside, and his hands found the spot where her bikini panties rode high up on her hip. He hooked his finger around the elastic and she shivered with surprised pleasure when he started to drag it down her thigh.

She released his shirt and smoothed her hands down his chest until she got to his belt. Lingering there for a few moments, she toyed with the buckle, and smiled when she felt his reaction in the deepening of the kiss.

"Keep that up and we will end up at my house," he murmured against her mouth.

"You won't hear me complain."

Moaning, he lightly bit her lower lip.

"Hey." She cupped his bulging fly. "How's that for—"

Behind them, someone cleared their throat, at the same time a circle of light bounced on the table and then streamed up to Evan's face. "Mighty cold out here for a picnic, isn't it, folks?"

Evan turned red. As discreetly as possible, he lowered his hand from under Liza's skirt. "Good evening, officer," he said evenly. "Anything wrong?"

The police officer shone the light in Liza's face. She raised an angry hand to block the glare. "That isn't necessary."

He wouldn't move the light away from her face. "What are you two doing out here?"

"Having a damn picnic," she said. "As you've already pointed out."

"Liza, it's okay." Evan tried to take her hand, but she jerked it out of reach.

"No, it's not. He's harassing us for no reason." She stared at the older man. He was about the same age that her father would've been, and he had that kind of cocky grin that made her nuts. "Now that you've determined we aren't stealing any trees, you can leave."

He glared at her, one eyebrow going up in challenge. "ID, please, ma'am." He glanced over at Evan, who looked annoyed. "You, too, sir."

"No problem." Liza got up and had to tug her skirt down before swinging her legs over the bench to the other side. "My purse is in the car. And then I'd like your badge number."

"Liza, wait." Evan tried to catch her arm. "Come on."

She didn't look at him or the cop as she stumbled in the dark toward the car, grateful that she hadn't fallen flat on her ass. God, but she hated cops, especially older smug ones, who still drove cruisers because they couldn't manage to pass the lieutenant's exam so they took it out on everyone else.

The law was supposed to protect people. But the fine folks in blue protected each other first. No matter what the cost. Even if it meant sacrificing their spouses and children.

She opened the car door and found her purse on the floorboard. First she got out a pen. A recent gas receipt was the only piece of paper she could find. Then she retrieved her wallet and slid out her driver's license.

"Ma'am, have you been drinking?" The cop was right behind her, his flashlight in hand, and he shined a light in her face as soon as she turned around.

She battled the urge to slap the damn thing out of his hand. "I wish. Here," she said, shoving the driver's license at him and then moving out of the light.

He studied it for a long time, which no doubt was to make her squirm. Screw him. She'd get his badge number, and tomorrow she'd write a letter to his commanding officer. One thing she could still do was write a mean letter. Just the thought of it soothed her.

Evan joined them, carrying the bag of cold food and the blanket. He stared at her with a mixture of annoyance and curiosity, which only fueled her anger. He didn't understand. She didn't expect him to. She didn't *want* him to.

She got the pen ready, ticked off that her hands were shaking. God forbid anyone get the idea that she was scared. She was angry and she wanted them to damn well know it.

The cop looked up. "Ma'am, I'm sure you're aware this license expires today."

"What are you talking about?" She grabbed it out of his hand. "It doesn't expire until my birthday."

Frowning, the cop slid a brief look at Evan. "That's today."

Liza stared at the two men. "It is?"

THEY'D DRIVEN A COUPLE of miles out of the park and still neither of them had said a word. Evan rarely got angry. But given the last five minutes he was ready to take her back to her car and say adios. For good.

The way she'd reacted to the police officer had been so over-the-top, Evan had been both irritated and embarrassed. If she'd just cooled it, the officer would've been gone in a minute, and they could've resumed making out like a couple of silly teenagers.

The stunned look on her face when she'd realized it was her birthday leveled the playing field again. His anger had evaporated as quickly as it had sparked. How could she not remember it was her birthday? As much as he wasn't one to celebrate holidays, he at least knew when his birthday was. He also knew his parents' birthdays and each of his brother's. And if by chance he was busy the morning of the event and temporarily forgot, his mother would be quick to remind him. Didn't Liza have anyone to remind her?

"So," he said finally. "I gotta ask. How could you not know today was your birthday?"

She sighed loudly. "Half the time I don't even know what date it is."

"Well, happy birthday."

"Thanks," she muttered and continued to stare out of the passenger window.

"Why the long face? Is this the big three-o?"

That got her attention. She turned to give him a dirty look. "No."

He smiled. "It's no big deal. I'm halfway to forty myself."

"You're thirty-five?"

"Yep."

"Wow, I've never been out with a guy as old as you before."

"Very funny." He pulled over to the curb and threw the car into Park.

"What are you doing?"

He stretched his arm across the top of her seat, ignoring the cars that steadily whizzed by them. "What was that about with the police officer?"

Her expression turned into a petulant frown. "I don't like cops."

"You made a big thing out of nothing. He was just doing his job."

"He was unduly harassing us."

"He was reacting to you."

"You know what, it's none of your business." She folded her arms across her chest and angled herself toward the window.

"The hell it isn't. I was there, too, remember?"

At his raised voice, she turned back to him. "My dad was a cop."

"So you didn't get along with him, and now all cops are bad."

"My father wasn't just a cop, he was a drunk, okay?"

"I see."

Even in the semidarkness he saw anger flash in her eyes. "Nice, you probably did a rotation with a shrink during your residency and now you know everything about me."

"There you go again."

"What?"

"Treating me like the enemy."

"It's that superior attitude of yours."

His temper started to climb. "Explain that to me. How have I come off superior?"

She opened her mouth to say something, and then shut it again and looked away.

"You can't explain because it isn't true, but you can apologize."

She kept her face averted for a moment, and then pressed her lips together and slowly met his eyes. "You're right. I'm sorry."

He'd been ready to drive her back to her car, and then she'd caught him with an unexpected apology. This woman was going to make him insane. She was one contradiction after another. To keep seeing her would inevitably be asking for trouble. Ironically, that pretty much made her perfect. This was not a woman who elicited emotional involvement.

"This isn't an excuse," she continued, sounding defensive, "but the man who referred to himself as my father wasn't what you'd call a pleasant drunk."

"He hit you?"

"Came close a few times, but no."

"Your mother?"

Liza abruptly looked the other way and murmured, "She wasn't so lucky, and nobody seemed to give a shit."

Evan didn't ask anything more. He got the picture.

He knew more than he wanted to about adult children of alcoholics. For many, their early experiences lingered and governed their future decisions. Control was often a big issue for them. Liza had some baggage, all right. But hell, so did he.

"Just so you know, I'm not looking for pity," she said. "A lot of kids had it worse than I did."

"Good. I'm not offering any." He put the car back in Drive, and then pulled out into traffic.

Liza laid her head back and laughed softly. "You constantly surprise me."

"Is that good or bad?"

"I'm not sure yet."

He slid her a glance in time to see her smile. "Still hungry?"

"The food is cold."

After they'd gone three blocks, he turned onto Peachtree.

Straightening, she looked around. "Where are we going now?"

"My place."

6

RICK SHAKILY PUSHED himself up to a sitting position. He could see the digital clock if he squinted, but the red numbers were one big blur. The table lamp had burned out three days ago but he didn't have a replacement bulb.

Liza. Where the hell was she? The stupid bitch was supposed to take care of things like that.

A beer bottle sat at the edge of the coffee table. His mouth was so friggin' dry he couldn't even swallow. He grabbed the bottle and tipped it to his lips. Empty. He threw it against the wall between his and Liza's apartments. The *thud* echoed in the blackness, followed by the sound of glass flying everywhere.

He hoped it woke the bitch up. She had no damn business paying for a second apartment. He needed that money. She was getting stingier and stingier, not even picking up packs of cigarettes for him anymore.

"Hey!" he yelled at the wall.

Stumbling to his feet, he cursed when a shard of glass poked through one of his socks and cut him.

He made it to the wall and banged at it with the flat of his hand.

No sound from the other side.

"Hey!"

He banged again, hurting the hell out of his palm and nearly tumbling face-first onto the floor. Screw her. A carton of cigarettes sat on the kitchen counter. He needed a smoke. His heel caught on a jagged piece of the broken bottle and he yelped in pain.

"Son of a bitch."

Tomorrow he was going to talk to that damn lawyer himself. No more waiting for Liza's measly handouts. He knew she was lying to him. She had money. Her daddy had left her a nice insurance policy. Nice enough to keep Rick in smack until the real money came.

He made it to the kitchen, flipped on the light and opened a beer before fumbling for the cigarettes. The lighter slipped and bounced on the floor and he cursed. He didn't like the way Liza was acting lately. She was getting too mouthy for someone he was supposed to have by the balls.

He gulped down half the beer and then opened the nearly empty bottle of vodka. With one pull he finished it off, then wiped his mouth with the back of his hand. Shit. Something was different about her. She didn't jump anymore when he talked. Normally, he didn't have to ask for cigarettes or booze.

She always kept him supplied. Not now.

Maybe she planned on taking off with the settlement money. Screw him. Screw Eve. Shit.

The thought tore through him like a tornado. The stupid bitch. If she bolted…

He ran to the front door and jerked it open. The lights were off in her apartment. It had to be after midnight. Tough shit if she was asleep. They needed to talk. Now. He pounded on her front door.

"Liza!"

No answer.

He tried to peer into the window but the drapes were drawn too tight to see anything. He pounded at the door again. "Open up, bitch!"

Nothing.

A light came on from the apartment on the other side of hers. The door opened and a burly guy stood there naked, his face an angry red. "Shut the hell up, or I'll come out there and do it for you."

Rick backed away. He glanced down at the parking lot, scanning the cars for as far as he could see. No sign of her old compact. Didn't mean anything. She could've parked anywhere. But if she was gone, that cow with the kid might know where Liza was.

He hung on to the rail for support and stumbled to the end of the corridor. He wasn't sure if the end unit was the right one but he saw the kid playing there a lot. The apartment was dark, just like most of the others in the complex.

Pressing his ear to the door, he knocked lightly so he wouldn't piss off the naked guy. A light immediately came on. A second later, the door cracked open. Bingo. He had the right apartment.

With one fearful eye, the woman peered out at him through the crack. "What do you want?"

"Where is she?"

"Who?"

"God damn it. You know who I'm talking about."

The woman shrunk back.

"Who is it, mama?" Yawning, the kid tried to squeeze between her mother and the door frame. Her eyes widened when she saw Rick.

"Go back to bed." The woman cut her off. "Now." She turned to Rick. "I don't know where Liza is. It's late. Maybe she's sleeping."

She wasn't bad-looking up close. Except for the scar. Didn't matter. It had been a helluva long time since he'd gotten laid. Rick slid his hand in and hooked a finger under her chin. "You wouldn't lie to me, would you?"

Fear flashed in her eyes. She jerked away. "Go to hell!" she said, and slammed the door on his wrist.

"Fuck." He broke free and cradled his wrist with his other hand. "You stupid cow. You're going to pay for that. You and Liza."

Several more lights went on in other apartments, and he hurried back to his own. Friggin' Liza. No more sneaking off. From now on he'd follow her. She wasn't going to make a move without him knowing about it.

EVAN TOOK THEM to a part of town Liza didn't recognize. She'd only lived in Atlanta for about four years in a Midtown apartment that was only a few blocks from the studio. She'd worked long hours and rarely ventured past the local bar where they all congregated. But she was familiar with the posh suburb of Buckhead, a place where a practicing doctor who also consulted on a popular television series could afford to live, but this wasn't it.

The subdivision was nice enough, just not what she expected. Nor was the modest ranch-style house that Evan slowed down in front of. He turned the car into the driveway and used the remote control to lift the door to the two-car garage, which was neater and cleaner than her apartment, with a row of gardening tools hanging from a rack on the wall. Very middle American. *So* not her style.

But neither was biting the head off a police officer she didn't even know. God, what was wrong with her? She snapped in a second and she couldn't seem to control it. And what the hell was wrong with Evan? If he had a brain in his head, he would've dropped her off at her car. Why was he sticking around? Probably because deep down he was a loser. Just like all the other guys she attracted.

He inched the car forward and stopped when a red beam suddenly appeared on the wall in front of them.

"Pretty fancy," she said.

"Ingenious, actually. You don't want to know how many walls I've dented."

"You?"

"I have other good qualities," he said blandly and pressed the remote to lower the garage door before getting out of the car.

She got out, too, and followed him past two recently used dirt bikes stashed in the corner. "Are these yours?"

"One belongs to my brother." He opened the door to the house, reached in to flip on a light and then let her go first. "The housekeeper was here today so I'm safe."

At the sight of the clean, glossy tile floor, she sighed. "I want a housekeeper."

Evan smiled. "After living in dorms and shared apartments, I'd gladly spend my last dollar on a housekeeper."

Liza walked farther down the hall. The kitchen was on the left, the floor covered with more of the creamy-colored veined tile. Not just any tile, but the really cool twenty-inch kind. The cabinets looked like custom-made cherry and the appliances were all stainless steel.

"You cook much?" she asked, noticing the well-equipped island under hanging brass pots.

"Hardly ever." He came from behind her and threw his keys on the granite countertop. "Although I make a damn good tuna sandwich."

"Why do you have all this?" She wandered over to the bay window area where there was a glass table with four contemporary chairs.

"The appliances came with the house." He opened the refrigerator. "Gladys, my housekeeper, makes me meals about three times a week. What would you like to drink?"

"Surprise me."

"I hate that."

She turned to him, smiling. "What?"

He held the refrigerator door open and motioned for her. "Get your cute little butt over here and choose something."

With an exaggerated sway of her hips, she approached, smiling seductively. When she got to him, she leaned over to look into the refrigerator, knowing full well that in this position, her short skirt hid very little.

He didn't hesitate to mold his hand to her backside. "See anything you want in there?"

She did a wiggle under his touch, not sure who she was teasing more. "Hmm, let me see…"

He dipped his hand so that it was partially wedged between her thighs. Her panties grew damp as his hand moved. He slipped a finger under the elastic. She gasped and had to grab the door to steady herself.

"I found something I want," he whispered, his finger probing deeper.

She closed her eyes. It had been so long since she'd been touched like this….

The door started to move, threatening her balance, and she quickly opened her eyes.

Evan removed his finger and urged her to back up. She didn't want to—his exploration felt so good—but it happened fast, and then he closed the refrigerator door. He took her by the shoulders and forced her to face him. Then he slanted his head and kissed her gently on the mouth.

Her hands were free to explore and she found his bulging fly. He moved against her touch, but when she started to unzip him he stopped her.

"Come," was all he said, and took her hand.

They passed the living room, which was sparsely decorated, but centered on a state-of-the-art large-screen television. The short hall led to his bedroom...very masculine in shades of brown and rust. He had a TV in there, too, a small older model sitting on a very plain cherry dresser.

The bed was huge. Probably a California king, although she hadn't actually seen one before. Just knew it was big. The nightstands matched the dresser, each one holding a heavy brass lamp. On the right one was an elaborate-looking phone system.

He started taking off his jacket. "Good thing Gladys changed the sheets today."

"Why? Did you have another guest last night?" She watched him toss the camel jacket onto the dark wood-and-brass valet in the corner.

"What kind of remark was that?" He didn't look at all amused as he turned to face her.

"Oh, come on." She walked over and pulled his tie loose. "I guess that was my clumsy way of saying I know this is just about sex and that's okay with me."

He shook his head, his eyes staying fastened on

hers as she pulled the tie free and threw it in the direction of the valet. "You are a handful."

She smiled. "It hasn't stopped you yet."

His mouth curved in an unexpected predatory smile, and he grabbed her wrist when she went for his belt buckle. "It's not going to stop me now."

Liza sucked in a breath when he reached under her skirt and pulled down one side of her panties. She froze, totally caught off guard. "Why, Dr. Gann," she whispered breathlessly.

"Don't move," he said.

She couldn't if she wanted to. He let go of her wrist and she stood there perfectly still while he crouched and pulled the other side of her panties down until they were around her ankles. He didn't have to tell her to step out of them. Clutching his shoulders, she did it automatically.

"What about you?" she asked in a voice she didn't recognize.

He only smiled and ran his palms over her calves and then up past her thighs, pausing for a second before filling his hands with her fleshy buttocks. While squeezing gently, he took the hem of her skirt between his teeth.

She nearly fell backward. Luckily, she was close enough to the bed so that she wouldn't have ended up on her ass. Didn't he understand that there was a certain order to the way things went?

Not that she wasn't adventurous…far from it. But this wasn't a move she'd expected from him. Man, had she ever had a misconception about doctors. Obviously, they weren't all stodgy brainiacs.

He got the skirt up high enough and pressed a kiss right in a very sensitive spot. She felt the tip of his tongue and goose bumps chased up her spine. Her fingers dug into his shoulders.

"I see you're not a breast man," she said to ease some of the tension.

"I'm getting there." His hands moved up from her backside and he yanked her sweater out from her waistband.

"Hey." She shoved at his shoulders but he wouldn't back off. "I want your shirt off first."

"Too bad." He ran his hands up her back.

"Don't I get a say?"

"Nope."

She laughed. "That's not how it works."

"Relax, Liza," he said, carefully laying her back onto the bed. "You don't always have to be in control."

She blinked. "What are you imply—"

He cut her off with an all-consuming kiss. She hadn't even realized that he'd pushed her sweater up past her bra. That he'd unfastened the front hook and cupped her bare breast. Using his thumb and forefinger, he lightly pinched her nipple before putting his mouth on it.

Her whole body thrummed with excitement. She could hardly breathe. This man literally stole her breath away. He knew exactly what to do, and when to do it to drive her insane. It had to be because she was so starved for physical touch.

More than a year had passed since she'd been with a man. Rick. The thought was like an ice-cold shower. Made her want to gag.

She pushed Evan hard, catching him by surprise, then he rolled over onto the bed. His mouth wet, his eyes wary, he stared at her. "What's wrong?"

She wasn't going to let Rick ruin this. No way. "Take your shirt off," she ordered and when he didn't move, added, "I mean it."

One side of Evan's mouth slowly went up. "You want it off, go for it." He laid back with his hands clasped behind his head.

He looked way too smug. She'd fix that. She got up on her knees, letting her sweater fall back down and cover all the goodies. She paused, enjoying the disappointment on his face, and then she lifted the hem and pulled the sweater off. The unfastened bra was easy. A little shimmy and it fell down her back, leaving her naked from the waist up.

His lips parted, the struggle for control etched in lines at the corners of his glassy eyes, and he reached up to touch her extended nipple. She slapped his hand away. He met her gaze, a cocky smile starting to form.

That's okay. She wasn't through with him yet. She swung a leg over his waist and straddled him. The skirt hid nothing. His gaze shot to the prize. She reached behind and found his erection, still hardening under her touch.

Liza quickly figured that stretched back like this was exposing more than she'd planned. She thought to leave the position, but it was too late. He entered her with his finger, going deep in the slick wetness, and rubbing the nub that felt way too good this early in the game. She didn't want to come right away....

"Don't," she whispered. "Please."

He had her nether lips spread, his gaze fastened there, his fingers working skillfully. "Liza, you really want me to stop?"

She moaned. "I—I...don't want—" Oh, it was too late. She fisted the comforter and bit down on her lower lip as the sensations started to mount. As the spasms came faster, harder, without mercy, her entire body felt as if it were on fire. Her mind became so fuzzy she couldn't see.

Wave after wave of heat sluiced over her skin until she thought there'd be no reprieve. That she'd burn forever, and never be the same again. She opened her eyes. Evan's face slowly came into focus.

He withdrew his hand and started unbuttoning his shirt. She didn't move. Lethargy seized total control. She wanted to help him, but she could only watch him fumble with each button. When she realized he was wearing a T-shirt beneath his dress shirt, she had to suppress a giggle. Of course he would be properly dressed. This was Evan.

"You could help," he said.

"I don't know. You wore me out."

He groaned. "I better not have."

She freed the last button and then, noticing he was

distracted by her exposed crotch, she promptly got off of him. He sat up and got rid of both shirts while she worked on his belt and fly. He hadn't cooled down any, making the zipper difficult to maneuver, and she felt the earlier excitement returning.

No more power play. They both got totally naked. The sight of his toned belly and impressive hard-on got her juices flowing again. He wasn't overly muscled, but it was obvious he didn't sit on his ass all the time, either. His chest was nice, too. Just a little bit of hair and lots of definition.

She ran her palm over his pecs and one small brown nipple, and then down over the slight ridges on his belly. He didn't move until she went lower and traced his shaft. He tensed then and cupped her breast.

"A shame to be wasting this nice big bed," he whispered and did a flicking thing with her nipple that would totally let him have his way.

To her surprise, she was the one who insisted on pulling the comforter down and getting in between the sheets. He seemed to be ready to get down and dirty, screw the comforter.

She crawled in first, while he used the opportunity to rub his palms over her backside. She wasn't usually ticklish but he got her just so and, laughing, she hurried to the other side of the bed and flipped onto her back.

He slid in next to her. As if by magic, his hand ended up between her thighs. He got two fingers inside her before she could say anything.

"Hey." She wiggled away. "I have some exploring of my own to do."

"Be my guest," he said, lying back and kicking the sheets away.

Liza smiled. Such a guy. She took his thickness in her hand and watched his eyes close. She traced a finger around the smooth, silky tip and then under the rim. He looked as if he was having enough trouble keeping still, and when she touched the tip with her tongue, he nearly came off the bed. He murmured something she couldn't understand.

It didn't matter. She was getting carried away, too. She used the moisture from her tongue to pump him, slowly at first, but gaining momentum with her own arousal.

He reached up, curled his hand around her neck and pulled her down for a brief but blistering kiss. "Just a minute," he whispered against her mouth.

In an instant he'd gotten something out of the nightstand and was back, savagely taking her mouth while he took care of business. In another moment, he had her on her back, and slowly entered her. The strain of control was on his face, in the way his neck corded, how his biceps bunched.

She moved her hips upward, wanting to snap that control. Wanting him to plunge hard and deep inside her. But he stayed slow and steady, filling her nearly to completion, and then withdrawing again until she almost begged.

"Relax," he said softly. "Just relax."

"Are you crazy?" she murmured.

As he sunk into her again, he whispered, "Happy birthday, baby."

7

LIZA PULLED THE thick down blanket up to her chin and snuggled farther into the covers. Evan had his arm thrown around her waist but he was so sound asleep he wasn't bothered by her moving around. He stayed on his stomach, his stubbly chin close to her face as they shared the same pillow. A really great pillow. The dense kind that still managed to stay soft. She used to have one of those. Before she'd been forced to stay in a cheap fleabag apartment.

She opened her eyes and stared at his lashes resting on his cheek. She hadn't noticed how thick or long they were, or the tiny mole just at the corner of his eye. His hair was too short and, even now, after a night of rolling around in the sheets, wasn't very messed up. Across his shoulders was a scattering of freckles, which seemed odd because he really wasn't that fair-skinned. Ten to one he really hated them.

God, how different he looked right now. Nothing like the geeky man she used to see at the station over a year ago. He'd changed, or maybe she had.

As much as she wanted to just keep staring at him, she had more pressing business. A soft glow came from the master bathroom from the night-light Evan kept in there. Earlier, she'd teased him about being afraid of the dark. Now she was glad for the beacon showing her the way in the unfamiliar room.

She slowly moved Evan's arm from around her waist, and then inched her way toward the other end of the bed. Parts of her that she'd nearly forgotten how to use ached like crazy. Evan had reminded her. Boy, had he. The guy sure had paid attention in anatomy class.

There wasn't an ounce of inhibition or modesty in the man's genes. He'd surprised her over and over again. For hours. Stamina was another one of his attributes. She had him totally wrong. Well, not totally. He was a little obsessive about keeping things in tidy rows. She smiled. Must have driven his college roommates nuts.

Quietly she closed the bathroom door behind her. She flipped on the light and faced herself in the mirror. Ugly red marks marred the skin just above her right breast and on the side of her neck. Another beard burn claimed a spot under her ear. Damn, damn, damn. Just what she needed. Hopefully makeup would cover up the mark.

She turned on the water, waited until it was warm and then splashed her face. The air was chilly without Evan's body heat. She hadn't even done her business yet, and she couldn't wait to get back into bed with him. Who would've guessed he could be so energetic?

The trouble was, it wasn't just because he was a warm body. Last night, Evan had made her feel safe. Ridiculous, of course. She meant nothing to him. They were consenting adults who enjoyed sex. Period. No big deal. She doubted there'd be a repeat performance. In fact, if she were smart, she'd tell him this was it. He was too much of a distraction.

Although, one more night wouldn't hurt.

She hurriedly used the john and then turned off the light. She was about to open the door when she realized the night-light wasn't on. Yet light came from behind her. She turned around. Sunlight seeped through the frosted glass window.

Shit.

It was morning.

She quickly collected her clothes and purse, and then called a cab before she got dressed.

LIZA GOT TO HER attorney's office, her legs still shaking from the scene with Rick. Half an hour after she'd gotten home from Evan's, Rick had shown up at her door, yelling and screaming and demanding to know where she'd been all night. Good thing one of the neighbors had threatened to call the cops. That had shut him up fast. But he wasn't done with her yet. She knew that all too well from past experience.

No more sneaking out. No more seeing Evan. He was a nice guy, and he had amazing hands that made her forget. But Rick was becoming more volatile and she couldn't afford him finding out about Evan. He didn't deserve being Rick's target. And sadly, she didn't deserve someone as nice as Evan.

She shut off the engine and noticed that the gas was close to the empty mark. Great. Just great. She'd used nearly all her cash on the cab from Evan's house to her car. Sighing, she climbed out and smoothed her sensible wool slacks. It hadn't been easy to get Kevin Wade to take her case. She knew he'd thought she was some kind of crackpot at first. The least she could do was look like a normal person. Maybe he'd even have good news for her today.

The offices of Kregel, Fitch & Devine were on the twelfth floor. Liza swore the damn elevator had stopped at every floor before she finally got to theirs. Topping things off was the big Christmas tree sitting in the middle of the foyer. God, she couldn't wait for all the holiday crap to be over.

Recognizing her immediately, the receptionist picked up the phone and called for Kevin's secretary. Liza had made a total pest out of herself for the past two months, and pretty much everyone on the floor knew her.

Too bad.

"Just go on back, Ms. Skinner," the receptionist said, and then went on with her typing.

Liza followed the corridor toward Kevin's office. Along the way were numerous other offices belonging to junior associates. She got two doors down from Kevin's office and heard a familiar voice. Talking to an older woman was Jenna Hamilton, CATL-TV's attorney. She was the same attorney being used by Eve and Jane and the rest of the lottery winners.

Did this mean good news? Was there another offer on the table? Liza's heart pounded as she entered Kevin's office. He looked up from his computer screen and smiled. Unfortunately, not a good-news kind of smile. She took a deep breath.

He motioned to the brown club chair opposite him. "I have news."

"Yeah?" Hope soared again.

"We have a court date."

"Oh. I thought— I just saw Jenna Hamilton."

Kevin shook his head. "That was nothing to do with your case."

"They aren't countering?"

He narrowed his dark brown eyes on her. "What counter? You flatly refused their offer."

"I know that." She put two fingers to her throbbing temple. Too little sleep. Too much stress. "I just thought maybe they'd come up with another amount."

He leaned back in his chair and looked sternly at her. "You can't have it both ways. You told me you were firm on the seven-way split."

"Right." She cleared her throat. How could she possibly be offended that Eve and Jane weren't willing to settle, or that they were willing to drag her to court? What irony. To them she was no longer a friend. She cleared her throat again. "When's the court date?"

"On the twenty-second."

"Of this month?"

He nodded.

Her pulse raced. "Is it good to go before a judge so close to Christmas?"

"It could go either way. But you told me you wanted this over with as soon as possible." He paused. "Your friend Rick called."

"He what?" Oh, no. She'd been careful not to leave a business card around, hoping he'd forgotten the law firm's name. But she'd underestimated him. This was bad. He was getting desperate. She had to watch herself, not give him a reason to be suspicious or feel insecure. "When?"

"Yesterday."

"What did you tell him?"

"Nothing, of course. He's not my client. You are." Over his long brown steepled fingers, Kevin regarded her with a kindness he hadn't shown before. He didn't have to tell her that Rick had been angry and vile. "The man is a liability to you, Liza. I recommend he not be in court with you."

Anger, sarcasm, hatefulness—all of that she could take. But not kindness. She lifted her chin. "I hope you didn't call me all the way over here to tell me that."

He smiled. "Actually, I wanted to see for myself how you're holding up."

"Yeah?" What nerve. She got to her feet.

"You're a wreck."

"Thank you."

"I'm serious, Liza. You don't want to go into court looking like some desperate druggie who dropped off the face of the earth for nearly a year, and then pops up and sues her friends."

She winced. "I don't do drugs."

"Appearance is everything. Dress smart, look alert. Take care of yourself."

She swallowed. Okay, so she'd been up all night. Lost a few pounds. None of his business. Self-consciously she raked a hand through her hair. There were so many tangles she couldn't get all the way through. "I'll be fine," she said. "You just worry about winning the case."

BAD ENOUGH SHE HADN'T left a note yesterday morning when she snuck out of his house, Evan still hadn't heard from Liza.

If she'd wanted, she could've easily contacted him yesterday at the studio, or even been waiting in the parking lot. But she'd chosen to leave him hanging, and he was getting more than a bit irritated over her rudeness.

Hurt, really. The sex had been great. He really felt as if they'd connected on some level. He'd been moved that she'd even confided in him about her father. And then, poof. The disappearing act.

"Dr. Gann?"

He looked up from the chart he'd been reading in his office. Normally his desk was organized and nearly spotless. Today it was a total mess of folders and journals. He hadn't even hung up his jacket. It lay across one of the black leather-and-chrome chairs sitting opposite him that were used for patient consultations.

"Is something wrong?" Betty asked with concerned blue eyes. She'd been his nurse from day one. He'd played tennis with her husband numerous times, and he'd even been to her kids' birthday parties. Other than his brothers, she was as close to a friend as he had.

But he couldn't tell her about Liza. Betty would get excited and want to meet her. That wouldn't happen. "Just a little tired. What's up?"

Her frown told him she wasn't convinced but all she said was, "The lab work came back for Mrs. Gardner. You might want to have a look at it before lunch. Her appointment is in two hours."

"Lunch?" He looked at his watch. It was already after two.

"I can order something for you."

"No, I'm not hungry." Damn, he'd planned on sneaking out for an hour. Try and catch Eve. See if she had Liza's cell number. "What have you got?"

She handed him the lab results and went to the door. "Oh, I almost forgot," she said, turning around. "A woman called earlier, she's not a patient…"

His entire body reacted. His pulse raced, his palms started getting clammy. *Liza.* Finally.

"She was hoping to get squeezed in today. Carolyn Sager recommended her."

"Anything serious?"

She smiled. "No. And I told her you had a tight schedule. She's coming in next week."

"Thanks. I'd like to get out of here by five." He went back to scanning the lab results, effectively avoiding Betty's inquiring look. She knew he didn't have a life. Normally he'd stay until seven, if necessary.

Not tonight. He had to figure out this thing with Liza. He seriously had no clue why she'd ditched him like this. If something had happened, or if she just wasn't interested, he wanted to know. Eve might be able to enlighten him. In fact, he had quite a few questions for her.

"I'M GLAD YOU CALLED," Eve said, gesturing for him to sit. "Or you would've missed me. As it is, I'm sorry but I only have ten minutes." She was pretty and charismatic, with a dynamite smile, and he could see why her show had become such a huge success.

Yet Liza was the one who'd caught his eye from the beginning. No explaining it. His lab partner in medical school would have explained the attraction as pure chemistry. Evan didn't buy that stuff.

"As I told you on the phone, I wanted to talk to you about Liza," he said, accepting the seat she offered.

She gave a small nod of her head, her face perfectly masked, except for the sadness in her green eyes she failed to disguise. "I'm not sure I can tell you much. I haven't seen her for some time."

"I know. She told me."

One of her eyebrows went up. "You've talked to her."

"We've met for dinner or drinks a couple of times this week," he said.

She blinked, surprise written all over her face. "How did that happen?"

"I saw her out in the parking lot one afternoon, and we got together."

Eve pressed her lips together and looked away, but not before he saw the hurt in her eyes.

"I think she was waiting to see you," he offered. "That day in the parking lot."

"I doubt it. We have nothing to say to each other."

"You were friends for a long time."

"Since we were eleven. Apparently that means nothing to her." Eve turned back to him, anger replacing the hurt. "Did she send you here?"

"No." He wanted to laugh. "Actually, I'm trying to find her."

"She pulled a disappearing act on you, too?" She shook her head and sighed. "Don't expect much. She has a habit of doing that."

"I guess that means you don't have her phone number."

She looked at him as if he'd asked her to moon her audience tomorrow. "Since I have nothing to say to her, no, I do not."

"I think she's in some kind of trouble," he said, watching her closely. Despite her attitude, Eve wasn't nearly as angry as she was sad and disappointed.

She blinked and opened her mouth to say something, but quickly shut it again. She looked down at her hands, absently shaking her head. "I have to go."

"Tell me what happened to split you guys up."

She warily raised her gaze to his. "Didn't you ask her?"

"You know Liza."

She started to smile and then sighed. "Honestly, I don't know. The show was going great, largely because of her creativity. Then one day we disagreed on a segment, like we'd done many times before, and she blew up. Stormed out of here like we'd personally attacked her. I didn't call her, or anything. That was a Friday. I figured she'd cool off and everything would be okay by Monday morning."

"You never saw her after that?"

With a bitter laugh, she said, "Not until after the lottery win." Then she turned pensive. "If she's in trouble it's because of Rick."

"Rick?"

"Her boyfriend. He was trouble from day one but Liza couldn't see it. Toward the end we thought he was maybe using some kind of drugs, even drinking a lot."

"She said she isn't seeing him."

"I sincerely hope you're right." She got to her feet. "I'm sorry. I really do have to go."

He stood, too. "Thanks."

"You might try her attorney, Kevin Wade." She walked him to her office door. "He'd know how to get ahold of Liza."

"Right. Thank you."

"I don't know his number but he's with Kregel, Fitch and Devine," she called after him.

He was already headed down the hall, fishing his cell phone out of his pocket.

LIZA FOUND A PARKING SPOT right near the stairs to her apartment and pulled out her bag of groceries. If Rick saw her car there and thought she'd stayed home all night maybe he'd back off. The ordeal was almost over. Two more weeks and a judge would decide her fate. She was so damn tired that no matter what the outcome, she was getting to the point that she'd just be glad when it was over.

"Hey," Mary Ellen called out when Liza was halfway up the stairs. The woman was leaning over the railing, her voice lower than usual. She pointed to her apartment and then motioned for Liza to follow.

Liza's gaze automatically went to Rick's window. It was too cold to be open. He was probably listening for her. Waiting to finish what he'd started earlier. She wasn't in the mood. Even though he'd be pleased with news of the court date, and it might even shut him up for a while, she just didn't want to deal with him right now.

She quietly ascended the stairs and went straight

for Mary Ellen's apartment. She stood in the doorway, looking fearfully toward Rick's room.

"What's wrong?" Liza asked, her head starting to pound.

Mary Ellen put a finger to her lips and quickly went inside. Even though the place was so tiny, it was immaculate. No toys laying around or dirty dishes sitting on the counter. The bed had been returned to being a sofa and the pillows were stacked neatly in the corner.

As soon as she shut the door behind Liza, Mary Ellen said, "He was looking for you night before last."

"I know." A sick feeling gnawed at her gut. "Did he come here?"

Mary Ellen nodded. "He thought I knew where you were."

Liza muttered a curse and then took the other woman's hands in hers. "I'm so sorry, Mary Ellen."

"It's not your fault." She shrugged her slim shoulders. "He didn't hurt us or nothing. Billy Ray over in twenty-one threatened to kick his ass and he took off real fast." A small smile lifted the corners of her lips before she frowned. "But he's really getting worse, Liza, and I'm afraid he's gonna hurt you."

"He won't." She gave her hands a final squeeze. "I promise."

"You can't make that promise," Mary Ellen said, solemnly shaking her head.

"I won't give him a reason to be mad, okay? Anyway, it's almost over."

"What is?"

"Look, in about two weeks he'll be moving out." Either way, no matter how the lawsuit's outcome was determined, she'd be done with him. She didn't want any of the money. She just wanted him gone.

Mary Ellen's sad eyes widened. "And you?"

"Me, too."

She shook her head. "But you're the best friend I've ever had."

Liza's heart broke a little. They were hardly friends. "We'll keep in touch, silly."

The door opened and both women jumped.

"Is it time for dinner yet?" Freedom's face was red from the cold, yet all she had on was a sweatshirt. "Hi, Liza."

"Close the door, honey," Mary Ellen said, already on her way to lock it.

"It's okay." The girl took off her red ball cap. "He's still passed out."

Liza exchanged glances with Mary Ellen. This kid was only eight. She shouldn't even know those two words. Although at that age, Liza had known the term all too well. God forbid Freedom grew up to be a mess like her. "Look," Liza said softly. "Next time you call the police."

"I don't have a phone," Mary Ellen reminded her.

"Here." Liza dug in her purse for her cell. She found her wallet and her sunglasses. Breath mints and a nail file. A hard candy had come unwrapped. She sifted through everything a second time. No cell phone.

It had to be here. She checked again. She'd had it just this morning before going to the store....

Oh, God. The last time she remembered having it was in Rick's apartment.

8

EVAN SAW HER CAR parked in the lot as soon as he left the station the next day. She hadn't returned his call, but that didn't matter now. He should be angry. And he still was a fraction. But he wanted so badly to talk to her. Find out what had gone so wrong that she'd sneaked out of his house.

He got halfway to her car when she opened the door and got out. After glancing over her shoulder, she turned to glare at him, her face flushed. As he got closer, she met him partway between a late-model black BMW and a midsize SUV.

"What the hell do you think you're doing?" she asked, her voice low but furious.

"Liza…"

"You had no right contacting my attorney," she said, her hand shaking as she pushed the hair away from her face.

"Calm down, Liza."

"Don't tell me to calm down."

He reached for her hand, but she jerked away. "All I did was leave a message with him."

"What made you think I wanted to hear from

you? The sex was great. Is that what you wanted to hear?"

"Jeez, Liza…" He looked around to see if anyone was within earshot. A couple of cameramen were walking toward them, but he didn't think they'd heard her. He couldn't see past the SUV. "Can we go someplace else to talk," he asked, angry now himself.

"There's nothing to talk about," she said in a lower voice, and then glanced over her shoulder. "It was a one-night stand. Get it?"

"Actually, I don't." At this point, he wasn't sure it mattered. She was a friggin' whack job. What had he seen in her in the first place?

"Please, Evan," she whispered, her lower lip trembling. "I can't do this."

He thought he saw her eyes well up, but she blinked and anything that might have been there was gone. That vulnerability was what kept him on the hook. She seemed tough one minute, and the next she looked as if she was going to shatter into a million pieces. "Liza, please tell me what's wrong."

She shook her head and backed up. "Nothing. I just have a lot going on right now."

He followed her to her compact. Something was wrong. The way she kept looking over her shoulder… She was afraid of something. Or someone. "Give me ten minutes," he said. "Just ten minutes."

"I can't do this, Evan. I cannot do this."

He put up his hands in supplication. "Okay."

Their eyes met, and he didn't mistake the regret in hers. "You're a good guy. I wish—" Shaking her head, she abruptly turned to the car door. And dropped her keys.

Evan moved quickly, snatching up the keys and then handing them to her. "If you ever need someone to talk to—"

Liza touched his hand. "You make this so hard."

"Good."

She almost smiled. "You're crazy."

"I thought I was boring."

Her lips parted, her brows lowered in indecision and then she briefly closed her eyes and shook her head. "I'm the crazy one," she muttered more to herself, and then said, "Let's go."

"Where?"

"I don't know. Anywhere." She glanced around. "Let's take your car."

"Sure."

"Come on." She spotted his car and hurried ahead of him.

He didn't know what the hell to think, but he'd figure it out later. He had to really move to catch up with her. "My house?"

"No."

He opened the car doors. "I have several other rooms besides the bedroom."

She gave him a small smile before slipping inside the car. "Take me someplace I've never been."

Evan laughed. "Am I allowed any hints?"

She laid her head back and closed her eyes. "No."

"Okay, then. I know just the place."

LIZA HAD TO BE OUT of her damn mind. If Rick woke up before she got home, he was going to go absolutely berserk. Mary Ellen and Freedom were safe. That was the main thing. Billy Ray had promised to keep an eye on them. The biker had to be three hundred pounds of muscle, with arms that were bigger than Liza's thighs.

Fortunately, Kevin had left her a message to call him instead of giving Evan her number. Rick had intercepted the voice mail before she could retrieve her phone from him and he'd blasted her with questions regarding what Kevin wanted. But none she hadn't been able to get around.

But the truth was, the smart thing for her to do was stay low for the next two weeks. Not give Rick any reasons to get suspicious or panic. That made him dangerous, and meant she should stay away from Evan.

What was it about him that made her get stupid? Or maybe it wasn't Evan. Maybe it was anyone with a dick. No, that wasn't true. She had no problem being alone, and definitely didn't have trouble telling a guy to kiss off. But Evan was different. He made her laugh. He made her feel safe. That in itself didn't make sense. Because there was no safe place. Not for someone like her.

"This time we're eating dinner," Evan said. "You like ribs?"

"Without the sauce."

He gave her a mock glare. "What kind of Southerner are you?"

"Technically, I'm a Yankee."

"Say it ain't so."

Liza smiled. "I was born in New York."

They came to an intersection and he stopped at the red light and looked at her. "I thought you were from Florida."

"We moved there when I was eleven. Before that we lived in Connecticut, New Jersey and Pennsylvania."

"All before you were eleven?"

She frowned at him. "Don't give me that look."

"What look? I was waiting for the light to turn green." Which it did at that moment and he made a left.

She let the conversation lag while she stared out the window. It was her own fault that he pitied her. She'd told him too much about her past, about her father. Evan wasn't stupid. He'd put two and two together. So many moves in such a short period of time all related to her father's drinking. And her mother's lack of backbone. Weren't mothers supposed to protect their children? Apparently Beverly Skinner had skipped that chapter from the parenting guide.

Liza laid her head back and sighed. She wasn't going to go there. All that would do was make her angry, or worse, horribly sad. She couldn't afford any negative emotions. She had to focus. Kevin Wade was right. She had to pull herself together before she went before the judge.

"You're quiet," Evan said, five minutes later.

"Enjoy it."

"I'd rather talk."

She heard the seriousness in his voice and wished she'd never gotten into his car. "I really don't have anything to say. I'm just trying to de-stress."

This time he lapsed into silence. After a few minutes, he asked, "I talked to Eve."

"When?"

"Yesterday afternoon. I thought she might have a phone number for you."

Just hearing Eve's name was like a knife in the heart. She and Jane's friendship had been the only truly good thing that had happened to Liza. And she'd allowed a man to destroy that. She wasn't even worthy of their friendship.

She swallowed around the lump in her throat. "Why in the hell would you think that?"

"Because you were friends."

"*Were* being the operative word." She couldn't take it anymore. Next time he stopped she was going to get out. Run as fast as she could.

"I think she misses you."

"Drop it."

Neither Eve nor Jane missed her. How could they? They thought she was the scum of the earth, and she didn't blame them even the tiniest bit. She was the one who missed them. Terribly. The irony was that she'd always depended on herself, handled her own problems, but if she'd ever really been up against the wall, it was Eve or Jane that she'd go to for help. This was the biggest mess of her life, and she didn't have a soul to turn to.

Evan pulled the car up to a curb behind a long line of cars and trucks. They were in a neighborhood she didn't recognize and not a particularly great one. Mostly there were houses one after another, a convenience store on one corner and a gas station on the other. Was he taking her to a party? That would be absurd.

"I think this is as close as we're going to get. Good thing it's unseasonably warm tonight." He shut off the engine, and then glanced down at her feet. "Tennis shoes. Good."

"Where are we?"

"You're going to like it. Trust me."

"Trust you?" Was he kidding? She didn't trust anybody. Not anymore.

"Can you do that?"

She looked into earnest brown eyes, remembered how good she'd felt in his arms. She couldn't let her guard down again. "Let's go."

"Wait."

Her hand on the door handle, she warily looked at him. She didn't want to talk anymore. It was way too easy to talk to Evan, and she didn't want anything slipping out that she might regret.

Cupping a hand around the nape of her neck, he leaned in and pressed his lips coaxingly against hers. She didn't want to give in. Still, this was better than talking. Better than just about anything. His mouth was warm and minty and his skillful tongue made it difficult not to participate.

She leaned closer and placed a hand on his thigh for balance. He shifted and her finger grazed the bulge straining his fly. He slackened his hold at the back of her neck and drew his hand over her shoulder and down the side of her arm. When he got to her hand, he covered it with his and, interestingly, was the one who broke the kiss.

"I've been waiting two days for that," he whispered and then briefly kissed her again before retreating.

"Glad you got it off your chest." Her glibness was undermined by the shakiness in her voice.

He smiled, and she turned away and exited the car.

"I hope you're not taking me to a party," she said after he came around the car and they started down the sidewalk. None of the houses looked as if they were especially rocking, but she couldn't see where else they'd be heading to.

"You're supposed to trust me, remember?"

"Those were your words, not mine. I don't trust anybody." She looked away from the disappointment that flickered in his face. She wasn't responsible for how he felt. Not her job.

They walked for a full block in silence, and then

crossed the street and kept walking. She'd be lying if she said that she wasn't intrigued. Although knowing Evan, they were probably going to a book club discussion or a poetry reading. Nothing wrong with either one. But definitely not her style.

Liza's thoughts went back to Eve, and whether she'd mentioned Rick to Evan. She'd give just about anything to find out how that conversation went. To know how much dirt Eve had given up about Rick, and about what a damn fool Liza had been to put up with his arrogance. Well, she'd give almost anything. Not her pride.

By the time they reached the middle of the next block she saw a house at the far corner, sitting by itself, that was ablaze with lights. Even the trees flanking the driveway had small white lights spiraling up their trunks. Several groups of people milled around the front yard. Behind the house, smoke filled the air. As they got closer, she caught a whiff of grilled meat.

She looked over at Evan.

He was watching her, a smile playing at the corners of his mouth. "It's not a party. It's part rib joint, part bar. Very public."

"Afraid I'm going to attack you?"

"Yep."

"You wish."

"Yep."

Liza grinned. "Seriously, a restaurant out here in the middle of a neighborhood?"

"Not exactly. We had to park back there because

I knew we wouldn't get a closer space. But the house sits on the main drag," he said, pointing at all the cars going by on the other side.

"I bet the neighbors are happy."

He shrugged. "Poor zoning. I know I would've moved."

Liza smiled at his blasé attitude. "Here I thought you were a Republican."

"Maybe I am."

"Hey, Evan." A man holding a bottle of beer saw them approach the driveway. "Eric's been looking for you."

Evan lifted his chin in greeting. "Out back?"

The guy nodded and then returned to his conversation with two blond women who apparently weren't bothered by the chilly air, either, judging by their cute skimpy dresses.

Liza dismally glanced down at her old faded jeans and ratty black sweater. She hadn't planned on going anywhere, much less someplace with Evan. Hell, what did she care? She wasn't trying to impress Evan or anyone else. Tossing her hair over her shoulder, she lifted her chin as she walked alongside Evan into the house.

What apparently once had been the living room was a mass of tables and chairs, not necessarily matching. At some point there had to be a wall separating the kitchen from the living room, but it had been knocked down and the two-person manned kitchen was now divided only by a counter, crowded with plates of potato salad, coleslaw and

French fries. Sticking out from under each plate was an order ticket.

The noise level was high and annoying, and nothing like she thought Evan would appreciate. But he apparently came here often enough that five people had greeted him by the time they made it to the back door.

He'd introduced her each time, and each time the person looked surprised. The way she was dressed had nothing to do with it because as dumpy as she looked, mostly everyone else was in jeans, too. Made her wonder how often he brought a date with him.

He opened the back door, and they walked into a large enclosed patio. In the corner was a three-man band playing eighties rock. Not too loud, just enough so that you could actually enjoy the music. The rest of the floor was taken up with picnic tables. Beyond the enclosure were more wooden tables where groups of people sat, drinking beer, laughing and talking. Around the side of the house, two men stood over split barrels, turning slabs of ribs over an open fire.

The place was crowded but Evan steered her to an available table to the right of the stage. They received several interested looks as they weaved their way across the patio, and then she realized it was because everyone seemed to know Evan.

They'd only sat down for a few minutes when a dark-haired waitress wearing jeans and a tight, lime-green T-shirt brought them two light beers.

"Hey, Doc," she said, setting the bottles on the table and then wiping her hands on her jeans. "You eating?"

"Later." He turned to Liza. "Okay with you?"

"Fine."

The woman sized her up. "Been here before, honey?"

"Nope. I'm a virgin."

The younger woman's throaty laugh sounded like a two-pack-a-day habit. "I'll bring a menu then check back with you later, Doc."

Liza watched the waitress go to an old refrigerator in the corner and take out five beers that she loaded on a tray. "How did you find this place?"

"I've been coming here for years. By the way, they have wine and soda if you prefer."

"No, beer is good." She tipped the cold bottle to her lips.

"If you want a glass you have to ask for it. The glass will be clean, the look will be dirty. They're big on low maintenance."

"Amen to that."

He reached across the table and touched his fingertips to hers. "Why don't you come around and sit on this side with me?"

She gave him a teasing grin. "Then how can I gaze into your eyes?"

"I'll give you something else to gaze at."

"Ooh, I like it when you're naughty."

"You want to see naughty? Get your sweet little backside over here."

"I dare you."

"You won't know until you get over here."

Liza laughed. She wasn't so sure he wasn't serious. The more she saw of Evan, the more she believed she truly didn't know this man. That wasn't totally true. She knew the important stuff. That he was kind and patient and understanding, and that he had a great sense of humor. But there was this other side to him, a side that contradicted the doctor image.

Maybe it was her own biased opinion of the type of person she thought would become a doctor. The kind of student in college who practically lived in labs and libraries, while she'd been hitting every party and club that would overlook her lousy fake ID. If a guy rode in on a bike, Harleys being her favorite, the odds were three-to-one she'd be riding home with him. She'd liked them rough and tough, screw the guys that cultivated their sensitive sides and wanted to explore their feelings.

"What do you think of the music?" Evan asked, breaking into her thoughts.

"They're good. Just my kind of music." She smiled at him, got up and went around to his side. "Move."

"Yes, ma'am." He slid over but didn't leave her all that much room.

She reached across the table for her forgotten beer and then slid in beside him, pressing her thigh to his. She gave him a nudge with her hip, and he surprised her by picking up her hand and kissing the back of it.

"It's okay that I sit on the outside then?" she asked, liking that he held on to her hand.

He frowned slightly. "Now that you mention it…"

"I'm not moving."

"Good," he whispered, his gaze on her lips.

She thought he was going to kiss her, but then the band stopped playing and he looked toward the stage. She turned, too, but all she saw was the band members putting down their instruments.

The long-haired drummer left the stage and headed toward them. He slid onto the bench she'd vacated, glanced at her and then said to Evan, "About time you got here, bro."

"Liza, this is Eric."

"I've heard about you," Eric said before she had a chance to say anything. "Glad you could make it. Sorry I'm gonna have to steal your date." He turned back to Evan. "I need you for about an hour."

"Forget it."

Liza finally remembered who Eric was—he was Evan's brother. Even if she didn't know, the melting brown eyes gave it away. But there, any similarity ended. Eric was taller and lankier and hadn't picked up a razor in at least a week. His jeans were torn and his Grateful Dead T-shirt was a size too small, although it showed off surprisingly hunky biceps. Back in the day, if Liza had met him at a party she'd have been all over him.

"Come on," Eric said, and then took a sip of Evan's beer. "Just until Tony gets here. You know I'm not so hot on the drums."

A blonde wearing black leather came up behind him and slid her arms around his neck, her fake platinum-blond hair spilling over his shoulders. She lowered her red lips close to his ear. "You sounded good to me."

Eric didn't look thrilled. "I'm talking to someone here."

"Can't I sit with you during the break?" she asked and snuggled up beside him before he could answer.

"Later, Stephanie."

She sighed. "It's Melanie." Then she got up and wandered over to the bass guitarist.

The scene made Liza's stomach turn. God, had she ever been that bad? No, she had more pride than that. Except when it had come to Rick.

"Liza," Eric said, "mind loaning him out for an hour?"

Evan exhaled sharply. "What part of no don't you get?"

Liza looked from Evan to his brother. "What's this about, anyway?"

Eric grinned at his brother. "Don't you wanna see the best drummer in Atlanta bring down the house?"

9

LIZA TURNED and stared at Evan. "You play the drums?"

He actually looked embarrassed. "Not really. A little bit."

Eric had just gotten a beer from the waitress. Chuckling, he uncapped it. "Damn near put himself through medical school playing the drums."

She blinked at him. "You did?"

"I was in a band." He shrugged. "We mostly played on weekends. I still worked a research job a couple of times a week."

"Would I know the name of the band?"

"I doubt it."

"Tell me."

He grimaced, clearly uncomfortable with the subject. "Messed Up."

She laughed. "Interesting."

"I was twenty."

"He could've stayed in the biz if he wanted and made some real dough," Eric said before taking another long pull.

"Yeah, unlike practicing medicine," Evan said dryly.

"I'm just saying. Everybody wanted you."

"Go play," Liza said suddenly.

He shook his head. "I want to have some dinner, then—"

"Come on," she said, putting a hand on his thigh and squeezing gently. "I really want to hear you play."

Evan's brows went up in warning.

Eric grinned. "Better go practice a few minutes. We're back on in fifteen."

Evan rose and shrugged out of his jacket. Liza took it from him and carefully laid it across her lap. "Even if Tony doesn't show up, I'm done after the set," he said, rolling back his sleeves two turns. "Got it?"

"Got it." Eric winked at Liza and then they watched him head to the stage. "I knew he wouldn't let me down."

Liza smiled at the fondness in Eric's voice. Must be nice to have a brother to depend on. "Where do you fall in the Gann pecking order?"

"In the middle. We have a younger brother. Elton's in his second year of law school."

"Wow. Talented trio."

He smiled, and she saw that was something else he shared with Evan. "I have a degree in English lit myself, but I never got around to using it."

"You Gann boys sure do surprise me."

"Yeah, wait until you hear my boy up there play. He's gonna blow your skirt up."

Again, the fondness in his voice and gaze tugged at Liza's heart. Envy wormed its way in there. She couldn't lose the petty feeling, even knowing that it was just as well her parents hadn't had any more kids to suffer their cruel indifference.

One of the other guys from the band motioned for Eric and he excused himself. She didn't mind sitting alone. She liked being able to watch Evan undisturbed. He was the only one of the group wearing short hair and a shirt that hadn't gone through one too many washings. Even though he looked out of place it didn't seem to bother him. She admired his confidence.

Eric produced another guitar, while a shorter, stockier guy tuned his bass. The singer, his sandy-blond hair nearly down to his waist, practiced his cocky smile on a bevy of big-busted groupies before joining the rest of the band.

A few minutes later when the set started with Miami Sound Machine's "Conga" she understood the reason for Evan's self-assurance. The guy was totally awesome. He was like a different person up there. The way he moved with incredible rhythm, the way he really got into the song, his expression a reflection of the lyrics.

She'd always loved music, mostly classic rock, but she wasn't a connoisseur by any stretch of the imagination. She just knew what she liked. And what Evan was doing up there…well, that certainly tipped the like scale.

If this whole evening had been orchestrated to turn her on, the attempt was a rousing success. By the fourth song, she had a good mind to yank him off that stage and drag him back to his house. When he did a solo, she just about melted into the bench. In fact, the hour seemed to go by exceedingly fast and when the last song for the set was announced, she wasn't sure if that made her happy or disappointed.

"You were fantastic," she said as soon as he joined her again. "How did you learn to play like that?"

"I got my first set of drums for my ninth birthday."

"And your parents didn't go crazy?"

"The rule was that I played only in the garage. I don't think my parents liked the neighbors on our left."

She smiled. "Tell the truth, were they sorry they bought them for you?"

"Not in the least. Come on, let's get some ribs." He signaled the waitress. "I worked up one hell of an appetite."

A few people stopped by the table to tell him how much they enjoyed his performance, and although he thanked them politely, he subtly let them know that he didn't want to chat. That all he wanted was to be with Liza. The warmth that spread throughout her chest and down through her belly ended quite predictably. But she doubted he'd want to skip dinner a third time.

The waitress came for their order and Evan explained that there were only two items—ribs or chicken, and each came with a choice of potato salad, baked beans or fries. Coleslaw, corn bread and pickles came whether you wanted them or not. With a snort, the waitress reminded him that a few people tried to talk her out of a couple of extra dill pickles from time to time. He gave her a smile that could melt butter, and she giggled like a schoolgirl.

After she left, Liza elbowed him in the ribs.

Evan jerked. "What's that for?"

"You charmer."

"You mean Colleen?" He glanced at the waitress who'd stopped at the next table. "She's a good kid."

"Kid?"

"She's still in college. To me that's a kid."

"You are old."

"Okay, I admit it."

"But not where it counts," she said, rubbing her hand against his thigh, her fingers close enough to the mother lode to make him smile.

"Is that an invitation?"

"I've always been a sucker for a drummer."

"Wish you'd told me earlier." He placed a restraining hand over hers when she got too bold.

Laughing, Liza withdrew. "I'm glad I met your brother."

"He's a good guy. So is the youngest one. Very smart. He has a bright future."

"Elton."

He looked at her. "You and Eric talked, I see."

"Some."

"What else did he tell you?"

She shrugged, curious at his intense reaction. Did he think Eric gave away family secrets? "Nothing, really. Only that Elton was in law school. Is anything wrong?"

"No, of course not."

"Oh, Eric did tell me he was an English lit major, which, I gotta tell you, surprised the hell out of me."

Evan smiled. "He surprised all of us. I think he'll end up teaching. But he's still young, single, no kids. Might as well do what he wants now."

"What about you?"

He didn't look at her. Just kept staring straight ahead at the stage, even though the band hadn't returned from their break. "What about me?"

"Ever get close to walking down the aisle?"

He didn't answer at first and she was beginning to think he wouldn't when he said, "Once."

"When was that?"

"Right after med school." He got distracted by something and craned his neck toward the patio door. "Good. There's Tony. He's their regular drummer."

A nicer person would drop the subject. "Were you actually engaged?"

"Yep."

"Are you going to tell me what happened, or do you want me to shut up?"

He stayed silent for a moment, and by the way his mouth and jaw tightened she could tell it wasn't an easy thing to talk about.

"Don't say a word. Forget I asked."

"It's okay. It was a long time ago, and it's certainly not as if I'm still in love with her. Any feelings I had for Angela died the moment I walked in on her and one of our friends in my bed."

"Ouch."

"Yeah, at the time."

Liza didn't know what to say. She kind of wished she hadn't asked. Although Evan didn't seem torn up about it. The original tension she'd detected was gone. His attention went to his brother, who'd just returned to the stage, along with the other guitarist.

"The funny thing was she still wanted to go on with the wedding," he said without a trace of bitterness. "She claimed it was just sex, that it didn't mean anything."

"Sometimes it is just about sex," Liza blurted, and then wanted to kick herself all the way back to Midtown.

Evan turned to look her in the eye. "But then, you don't talk marriage."

"True." Liza needed to just keep her big mouth shut. Everything was coming out wrong. Whoever that woman was had to be a complete moron. Evan would make a perfect husband. Not that Liza was in the market. "I didn't mean—"

He touched her arm, and then rubbed it with a familiarity that warmed her. Yeah, Angela was totally insane. "It's okay, Liza. That's what I admire about you most. You're up front about what you want. We know exactly where we stand. It is just about sex."

She forced a smile. He was right. Absolutely. So why did she suddenly feel so bad?

EVAN THREW HIS CAR KEYS on the counter, next to the mail his housekeeper had left for him. "Want something to drink?" he asked Liza.

Before he could turn around, he felt her hands on him. Her breasts pressed against his back, she slid her arms around his waist, and then went for the buckle.

"Hey, slow down." He turned to face her, and then intercepted her questing hands.

"Why?"

He lifted her chin so that he could look into her eyes. Something was wrong. He just didn't know what. The ride home had been quiet and he'd half expected her to tell him she'd changed her mind and wanted to be dropped off.

He smiled. "Dare I say we have all night?"

She blinked. "Damn." She walked away, looking restless suddenly.

"What's wrong?"

"I should have picked up my car."

"I'll take you back to get it anytime you say."

She paced the small kitchen. "Maybe I should go get it now."

"It's safe in the station's parking lot, not as if it's going to get towed."

She waved a dismissive hand. "I don't like being stranded."

"I'll try not to take that personally." He took off his sports jacket and laid it over his arm. "I'm going to go get a fire started in the bedroom. Come talk to me."

"Talk, huh?"

"Do anything you want to me."

Liza grinned, looking more like herself again. "Can I tie you up?"

"That one I have to think about."

"Can you see the headlines now?" She skipped a couple of steps ahead and turned to face him, backing her way down the hall. "Famous Atlanta doctor—"

"You blew it already."

"What?"

"Famous?"

"Your name is on the credits for *Heartbeat*. That makes you famous."

"Only according to my mother's bridge group."

"Still, it— Ouch." She backed into the linen closet door where the hall dead-ended. "You could've warned me."

"And ruin your story?" He motioned for her to precede him into his room on the left.

She did, but kept an eye on him over her shoulder. "Now, I forgot what I was going to say."

"What a shame." He went into the closet to hang up his jacket.

"It had something to do with the famous doctor being bound and taken advantage of for hours and hours by some insatiable nymphomaniac."

"Isn't that redundant?"

"I can change the story."

"No, no, I like that part." He unbuttoned his shirt and threw it in the wicker hamper.

She stood, leaning a hip against the door frame,

watching him. "Today was the first time I've seen you without a tie."

"That hurts. That really hurts."

Her eyes widened. "What?"

He grinned. "For the past three years I have rarely worn a tie to the station. A sports jacket, yes. Guess who obviously never gave me a second look?"

"Guilty."

"Make it up to me."

The slow curve of her lips said she knew exactly what was on his mind. She pulled off her sweater. Her bra was red and transparent, her nipples already firm. "What about the fire?"

He kicked off his loafers. They landed somewhere in the back of the closet. "I'll get to it."

One fast flick of the clasp and her bra was gone. She unsnapped her jeans but didn't unzip them. "If you're not going to let me tie you up, I should at least get to be the boss."

He had a difficult time dragging his gaze away from her perfect breasts. They were small but the way they seemed to tip up really got his attention. "I think you called the shots last time."

"You're complaining?"

"No, ma'am."

"Come here." She moved toward him, unzipping her jeans.

He did the same with his slacks and toed off his socks until all he had on were navy-blue boxers.

Liza got down to a red thong. At least that's what he thought the tiny triangle was. He'd never actually seen a woman wearing one before. As she reached for the top of the comforter, she gave him a backside view. Oh, yeah, definitely a thong.

She pulled the comforter halfway down and then stopped to look at him with mock displeasure. "Don't just stand there. Start the fire while I get the bed ready."

"Anything you say," he murmured and went to do her bidding. Although it was difficult to walk away from the view. He was already getting ridiculously hard, his defense being that men were visual creatures.

"Wait. Get rid of the boxers." Her gaze went purposefully down to his crotch.

"Yes, ma'am," he said, and slowly lowered the waistband, his cock immediately springing to attention. He kicked the boxers out of the way and then touched himself, cupping the weight of his arousal.

Liza moistened her lips. They were the same shade of pale pink as her nipples. "You play dirty and I'll have to punish you."

"That's supposed to discourage me?" He started toward her but she put up a restraining hand. "Oh, right. The fire." He found the switch on the side of the wall that turned on the gas and flipped it on. On cue, the flames sprung up.

She scoffed. "That's cheating. I thought we were going to have a real fire."

"Stick your hand in there and tell me it's not real." He pulled down the other side of the comforter, trying not to stare at her breasts.

"In the interest of time," she said, her gaze skimming his erection, "I'll let it slide."

He laughed. "Baby, I gotta tell you. I plan on doing a lot of sliding."

She tried not to smile, and abruptly turned away, which was perfect because he came up behind her and pressed his cock against her firm, smooth backside. She bent slightly, and rubbed against him, making him shudder. Even without saying a word she was still in control.

He closed his eyes and reached around to cup her breasts. As a doctor he saw a lot of naked bodies, but he'd never seen nipples quite like hers. When they blossomed they grew more than twice the normal size, as if begging to be touched and suckled. He loved the feel of them between his thumb and forefinger, and apparently she did, too, because she reacted with calculated hip movements that brought him too close to the edge.

He pulled her around to face him, and then kissed her deeply before she could protest. She wound her arms around his neck, her taut nipples teasing him as she pressed closer. He squeezed her buttocks, pulling her against his rock-hard cock.

A few movements of his own made her moan softly against his mouth.

"Stay the night," he whispered, and recognized the mistake when she tensed.

She slackened her arms around his neck. "Let's not get ahead of ourselves."

"No pressure. I just want to wake up with you beside me."

"Why?"

"Couldn't say." And that was the damn truth. Crazy as it was. Usually he felt the opposite. Small talk led up to the event, and after that it was "have a nice day." He wasn't a pig about it, but that's how it went.

She'd pulled back to look at him, her hazel eyes a stormy gray he hadn't seen before. "This is still just about sex, right?"

He nodded, although without his earlier conviction. Not that he'd changed his mind. Single life suited him. No expectations, no promises, no dreary routine. And he knew for sure Liza felt the same way. But saying it out loud again didn't feel right somehow.

She lifted herself on tiptoes and kissed him gently. "I promise I won't walk out without waking you."

"I promise to hold you to that promise."

"Don't worry. A taxi ride back to my place costs a fortune."

"Thanks." He pinched her bottom.

Liza laughed, and then pinched him right back.

"Enough horseplay." He scooped her up and dropped her on top of the bed.

She wiggled over toward the middle and he crawled in beside her. He took a nipple into his mouth, and she arched her back. Then he slipped a hand between her thighs. Good. She was as wet as he was hard.

10

LIZA RAN HER PALMS up Evan's chest, over his shoulders and as far as she could reach down his back. She loved the way his taut skin molded over each bone and muscle, how it dipped and curved and how his firm derriere filled her palms. His waist and hips were narrow, his shoulders broad even without his padded suit jackets.

Because she'd lost some weight—probably too much, judging by the way her old jeans had hung way down on her hips—she was self-conscious about how she felt to him. Her chest had gotten a little bony and her hip bones stuck way out even when she wasn't lying on her back. The loss hadn't been voluntary. Too much stress had seemed to change her metabolism. She hadn't given it too much thought until now.

"You look so serious." Evan lifted her chin. "What's the matter?"

"I was thinking how weird this is. You and me. You know?"

He moaned dramatically, putting a hand to his heart.

She took a nip at his lip. "You know what I mean. We've seen each other around the studio for over three years and nothing happened."

"I asked. You turned me down." He tweaked her sensitive nipple. "Remember that?"

"Hey." She got him back with a hard grip at the base of his cock. "Really?"

He looked grimly at her. "You don't remember?"

She shook her head. She wasn't going to lie. "It was a bad time in my life."

"Rick?"

She withdrew her hand. "Why would you bring him up now?" She moved toward the edge of the bed. "You just ruined everything."

"I'm sorry. I didn't know he was a touchy subject. I thought he was out of your life."

"He is." She looked back over her shoulder at him. "He is."

"Okay."

Liza took a deep breath. "I don't see him anymore. But he's still around."

"Don't run away, Liza."

She felt the bed dip behind her. And then his hand was on her thigh, rubbing, soothing. "I can't believe you remembered him."

"I didn't. Eve brought him up yesterday."

She jerked away from him and got to her feet; so they had discussed him. "This keeps getting better."

"I was only trying to find your phone number."

She reached for her bra and sweater. What the hell did she do with her jeans?

Evan came around the bed. He didn't have a stitch on and he was still semihard. Taking her by the shoulders, he said, "I think I deserve an honest conversation here."

"A reward for talking behind my back?"

"It wasn't like that."

"How the hell did Rick come up?"

"Eve said that if you were in any kind of trouble, it would be because of him."

"She never liked him." Her voice cracked. Damn it. "And she was right. Both her and Jane. They can gloat all they want. Who cares?"

"I doubt very much that's what they want."

She moved away. He didn't know crap about her life. About the hell she'd been through with Rick. "Where are my jeans?"

"Stop it, Liza."

She spun around to glare at him. "You stop it. I don't owe you anything."

The hurt mirrored in his eyes got to her.

"You're right. I thought maybe—" Looking resigned, he shook his head. "Absolutely right." He found her jeans and his slacks at the same time. "Here."

Liza took them, but she just stared down at her hands. What was wrong with her? Evan had been nothing but nice. He was a really good guy. Too good for her. "Evan, I'm sorry."

"No apology necessary." He scooped his boxers off the floor and stepped into them.

"Ah, dammit."

He frowned at her.

"Now, I just have to take those off again." She smiled seductively, but he wasn't having it.

"Sex isn't going to make this go away." He shook out his slacks.

She groaned in exasperation. "What is the matter with you? That is so not a guy thing to say."

That did get a slight smile. "Look, there's no reason not to at least have honesty between us. No strings to me doesn't mean I mess with a woman who's already taken."

"I swear to God, there is nothing happening between Rick and me. In fact, I despise the man." Was it her tone of voice? Her expression? Because she saw it in his face that he knew she was hiding something. "Rick is an asshole. He can't let go and sometimes he stalks me. That's why it may have seemed that I was acting oddly."

With heartwarming concern in his face he came to her. He put his hands on her waist. "What have the police done about it?"

She shook her head, feeling only slightly bad about the lie. Obviously she couldn't tell him everything, but he had to know there was nothing between her and Rick. "There's no proof. He's very sly."

"I know this detective—"

"No. Absolutely not. Getting anyone involved will only make matters worse."

Evan sighed, pulled her against his chest and hugged her close. "Is that why you need the lottery money? To get away from him?"

Being held like this by Evan felt too nice. He wasn't the solution to her problem. In fact, him knowing too much about Rick and the diaries could hurt her. "In a way."

"How can I help?"

"You're already doing that." She tipped her head back and waited only a second for his kiss. It lasted only another second.

"Liza, I want to help."

She put a finger to his lips. "Let's not ruin tonight."

He clearly didn't want to back off and the struggle in his eyes made her weak. Made her want to tell him everything. She tossed aside her jeans and slipped her hands under his waistband. He didn't argue when she slid the boxers down and then got rid of them.

She led him back to the bed, and then got in first, holding up the sheet and blanket for him to join her. He was already getting hard again and he'd barely stretched out when she reached for his cock.

She liked the hard, silky feel of him against her palm and cupped her hand around him. She pumped him slowly, just enough to get a low groan out of him. He briefly suckled each nipple, and just as she slackened her grip, he moved lower, and forced her thighs apart.

"Tell me what you like," he whispered.

"I think you've already figured that out."

He smiled, taking a long leisurely look, his gaze touching each breast, wet from his mouth, and then lingering on the triangle of hair at the juncture of her thighs.

First his fingers explored and taunted. She shifted, but he stayed with her. Finding it hard not to move erratically, she stretched her arms over her head, searching for the headboard and then grabbing hold of it.

He spread her legs even farther apart so that her ankles nearly reached the sides of the large bed. After he'd looked his fill, he used his thumbs to spread her even farther. His tongue scouted for the perfect spot, and each time she squirmed even the slightest, he put two fingers inside her. Not that the feeling wasn't heavenly, but it was as if he knew she was waiting for his tongue to make that connection. To tease the little nub that would bring so much pleasure.

He flicked his tongue over the spot and her bottom came off the bed. He slid his hands beneath her, squeezing the fleshy cheeks just the right amount to make her thrust upward. His tongue worked its magic until she didn't think she could take any more.

She didn't want to come yet. She wanted to play a while, so she used her grip of the headboard and pulled herself back out of reach. He looked up, confused, and she made her final escape.

"What's wrong?" he asked, sitting back on his haunches.

She saw that his arousal hadn't suffered from the setback. "Not a thing. As long as you remember who's in charge."

"Is that right?"

"I had a moment's lapse." She fluffed one of the pillows and put it back down. After scooting over to make room for him, she pointed to the pillow. "Here."

"Ah."

He crawled over, stopping to lave her right nipple. She should have stopped him. She was supposed to be in charge, but it felt too damn good. Finally, she shoved him away.

"Right," he muttered and flopped onto his back.

Liza smiled. "Poor you," she said, running her palm ever so lightly over his chest and down to his belly. "Is this so difficult?" she asked, using her wrist to brush the tip of his cock.

"No," he said in a forced falsetto.

She laughed. "I wonder just how sensitive these are." She rubbed the pad of her finger over one dark-brown nub, and then the other. They were already hard and responsive and his hands fisted at his sides. "Good boy. You keep your hands right there."

"Don't push it."

"Or else what?" She curled her fingers around his penis and squeezed gently.

His eyes briefly closing, he muttered an oath.

She moved down to where she could taste him. Her tongue replaced her hands, coursing up his shaft and then back down. She flicked the skin around the base. By the time she worked her way back up and drew him into her mouth, he could hardly keep still. She sucked him hard. He tried to reach for her but she held her ground.

She got between his thighs and, as he'd done to her earlier, she reached under his firm cheeks and held him right where she wanted him. Exploring him with her tongue only got her worked up. She really wanted him inside her. Filling her. Taking her to that safe place where she was untouchable. It was crazy. She didn't know him that well. But she couldn't deny how he'd made her feel in this very bed three nights ago.

Slowly, reluctantly, she released him. She slid her hands back around to use as leverage. Again he reached for her. But she was quick, and when he realized her intention, he laid back, his eyes mere slits as he gazed at her, his chest heaving. She saw the silver packet he'd left out on the nightstand just as she swung a leg over him.

She smiled. The good doctor was being responsible. She reached for the packet, tore it open and slowly unrolled the condom down his cock, making him shudder. For good measure, she pumped him a couple of times.

He moaned.

"Just making sure it fit," she said, laughing softly when he gave her a frustrated look.

"Now let's see how I fit." She lifted herself over him, holding his cock so that the tip just barely touched her. She wanted to sink down, ride him 'til he screamed, but then it would be over and she definitely didn't want that. Not yet.

She would take him to his limits and, in the process, the rest of the universe would vanish.

Evan moved his hips up, trying to enter her.

She smiled, closed her eyes and moved herself an inch away from him.

Ignoring his moan, she braced her legs more firmly on the bed, and braced his cock more firmly in her hand. He wasn't going anywhere she didn't want him to go. Right now, that meant skimming along her lips. Teasing, nothing more. He would feel her heat, the hint of moisture. He would be patient, but only for so long.

She reached behind her with her left hand. It was an awkward pose, since she wasn't letting go with her right hand. Bending back as far as she could, she tickled the inside of his thigh.

Obediently, Evan parted his legs, giving her access to her real objective.

He was a natural kind of man, not one of those poster boys who shaved every damn thing. Her fingertips played with his soft hair, then the softer skin of his balls.

He hissed, arching once more.

Retaliation was swift. Her hands left both holds, her thighs, feeling the burn now, lifted her away from any contact.

His curse was quite vivid, but she figured he was catching on. When he'd relaxed once more, she lowered herself, then with her right hand, she gripped him under the glans. With her left, she massaged him—quick flicks with each finger, fluttering, her nails brushing the tender skin in a soft legato.

"Liza, Liza," he repeated, but his teeth were clenched and it took her a few seconds to understand him.

"Hold on tight," she whispered.

She slid the crown of his cock inside her. She knew she was wet and hot, and that it had to feel amazing as she moved him back and forth.

His thighs, pressed against her own, started to tremble. She knew he wanted to thrust up into her. He'd get his wish…eventually.

Right now, though, she guided him to her clit. Increasing the pace of the rubbing, she started breathing harder, losing her rhythm as the sensations spread from between her legs to the rest of her body.

Sadly, she had to abandon her teasing. She needed her left hand to steady herself, to guide him away from her sensitized clit to a deeper victory.

Moving her hand down, she placed him a few inches inside, to where she could grip him not with her hand but with her vaginal muscles.

He arched again, but just his back this time. That, and he pulled the sheets so hard with his fists that they came off the mattress.

"Good boy," she said, her voice low and guttural.

"You're killing me."

"I would never do that," she said, but in truth, she wasn't sure she was strong enough to tough this out. Her body screamed for him to plunge, deep and hard, but all she did was squeeze and release.

Her hands were free again, and she wasn't sure

what to do with them. When she saw his gaze sweep over her body, the answer seemed obvious.

As she milked him, she took her nipples in her fingers. Not only did it feel delicious, she knew the view would make him crazy.

She squeezed her own flesh in counterpoint to squeezing him, although that only lasted for a moment. She had to synchronize—she simply didn't have the coordination anymore. Not as molten heat swirled inside her, bringing her to that sharp edge, that precipice, so close to coming she had to be careful.

Now, deeper. And a whole different kind of ride.

Tightening all her muscles, she lowered herself as slowly as she could until he was all the way inside. And then she stopped.

For a long moment, all she felt was the trembling of their bodies. All she heard was the deep, almost gasping breaths that filled the sex-scented air. A trickle of sweat snaked down her neck and she had to stop playing with her nipples because they were too sensitive.

He groaned and it turned into a growl. When he said her name, she realized time was running out. He was going to lose it. Or was that her?

She squeezed him once, then she rose up until she held him by just an inch.

"Please."

It was said so sweetly, she granted him his wish.

She lowered herself down, and with no hesitation, rose up again. The sensation of his upper thighs on the back of her ass, the way she shivered as he hit bottom…it felt beyond incredible.

Faster now, both of them panting, both of them thrusting. She moved only enough that each thrust rubbed her a new way, rubbed against her swollen—

It hit her like a giant wave, crashing her off balance. She gritted her teeth as she came explosively, as she heard him groan his own climax. She wanted to see him, to watch his face, but she couldn't open her eyes. Not until the quaking stopped.

Not until she found her breath. Until her heartbeat slowed to a hundred beats a second.

When she finally opened her eyes she couldn't see through her tears.

LIZA STARED AT THE FIRE, completely mesmerized. Shadows danced on the ceiling and walls. Amazingly, the gas fire made the room so warm they'd cast off the sheets and blankets. She looked over at Evan, sound asleep, lying facedown, the most perfect male butt in the whole world hers for the gawking.

He really did have a great body, but who would know it with him hiding under suits and sport coats. She'd really like to see him in jeans, she decided. Tight, worn jeans that couldn't hide a thing.

A flame shifted, its shadow licking the ceiling and drawing her attention back to the stone fireplace. When she was younger and hopeful, and life hadn't gotten in the way yet, she'd decided that her dream house would have a Jacuzzi in the master bathroom. She'd only been in one once. That first night she and her parents had moved to Jacksonville. The motel had screwed up their reservation, and after her father's drunken rants, the manager had put them in the honeymoon suite.

Looking back it was really a hokey motel, and the suite was hardly that, but at the time, Liza had thought she'd landed in paradise. The towels were thick…at least thicker than the threadbare offerings of the other motels they'd stayed in along the eastern coast. And there were two bars of soap, one for your hands, and one for the bath. Next to the sink there'd even been a free bottle of moisturizing lotion and shampoo. A big deal to an eleven-year-old who still wore last year's outgrown shoes.

But it was the Jacuzzi that had stolen her heart. Right off the bedroom, it sat in the middle of the tiled bathroom. You even had to walk up two steps to get inside the monstrous tub. It had been pure heaven, sitting in there, alone, with all those bubbles, the jetted water hitting her tired fanny after sitting on a suitcase in the backseat of her parents' sedan for ten hours.

Heaven fell apart when her father had walked into the bathroom and yanked her out of the tub. His handprint on her bare fanny lasted for days. She never did find out what had set him off that time. Her mother had taken her pills and was sound asleep. That they were prescribed, in her mind, sanctioned her addiction.

Liza changed her mind. Screw the Jacuzzi. A fireplace in the bedroom was totally the way to go.

"Hey." His voice was groggy with sleep and he barely had one eye open. "What time is it?"

She leaned over him to look at the digital alarm clock, and then sank back into the soft down pillow so that they faced each other at eye level. "One-thirty."

He threw an arm across her waist. "Tell me you don't have to go now."

She should. If Rick were awake… No. She wouldn't think about him. Not tonight. He'd already ruined enough of her life. "No, I don't."

He pulled her closer, and she gladly pressed herself against his side. His skin was so warm and smooth, but the possessive way he hooked his arm around her made her feel safer and more wanted than she ever had in her life.

"It's earlier than I thought," he said with a crooked smile, and attempted to raise himself.

She gripped his forearm, keeping him right where he was. "Go back to sleep," she said softly. "I'm not going anywhere." She kissed his shoulder. She knew he was tired, and he had to get up early to go to work tomorrow, but she didn't. "Let's both go back to sleep."

"Will you?"

She nodded. Even though in a few hours, she'd have hell to pay.

11

"NEXT TIME, HOW ABOUT you let me pick you up at your apartment?" Evan said after he got them on the road. As usual, he expected traffic to be brutal once he left the neighborhood and the extra ten minutes it would take to get her to her car was going to make him late for his first appointment.

When she didn't answer he looked over at her. She stared absently out of the window at the lineup of kids waiting for the school bus. At least now he understood why she was sometimes jumpy. He figured she was worried about Rick seeing them. Evan hoped like hell the guy did follow them one day. It would be the perfect excuse to get in the guy's face. Let him know what it felt like to be the victim.

Evan took one hand off the steering wheel to touch her arm. "Did you hear me?"

Slowly she turned to look at him. "This is really a nice neighborhood."

Evan sighed to himself. If she didn't want to talk about something, she was awfully good at changing the subject. Maybe he should leave it alone. Let her meet him anywhere she chose, and not bring up Rick. That was her business.

"No, seriously, the first time I came here I thought a doctor could do better than this. But I like it." She wrapped her arms around herself and shifted to watch a flock of sparrows perched on a bird feeder. "It feels homey. Happy. Even with all the leaves gone."

"I don't plan on staying here forever. But the price was right, and it suits me for now." Although he did like the older neighborhood with even older trees shading the houses.

"Come on, Doc, you make oodles of money. You could be living in Buckhead."

He smiled at the way she baited him. "Eric told you, huh?"

"Told me what?"

He shook his head. Her tone alone told him his brother had opened his big mouth. The tuition arrangement between Evan and his youngest brother was supposed to have been private, but somehow the whole damn family knew about it. "Elton's going to pay me back later by handling my malpractice cases."

"Malpractice? You?"

"You'd be surprised how many nuts are out there looking for a free ride."

Her silence spoke volumes.

"Liza?"

She dug into her purse and pulled out a pair of sunglasses. "Did I tell you I have a court date?"

"When?"

"The twenty-second."

"Of this month?"

She cleaned off the lenses and then slipped on the glasses. "Yep."

"Well, good." He nodded without enthusiasm. "Good for you."

Even with the glasses on he saw her disappointed frown. "Why do I suddenly feel like I'm sitting on the wrong side of the bleachers?"

"It's not that." If she won, she'd be gone before Christmas. No strings and all that, but he wasn't ready to watch her walk away.

"Right."

He'd never been so glad to see a traffic light turn red. With the string of cars in front of him, they'd inevitably sit through two lights. Taking advantage of the stop, he slid an arm along the back of her seat. "Haven't we been honest with each other?"

"I think so."

"Well, I have," he said, and waited for her to make the same claim. She didn't, so he added, "I told you that the lawsuit was your business. If I didn't sound like the cheering committee it's because I wanted to spend Christmas with you."

"Christmas?"

"Yeah, Christmas."

"I thought you hated Christmas."

"I'm not crazy about the holiday but my family always has this big dinner…."

She stared at him, as if waiting for him to finish.

It was gonna be a long wait. She could figure this one out. Finally, with a look of disbelief, she asked, "You want me to go with you?"

"Would that be so terrible? You've already met Eric."

She wrinkled her nose. "But I'd have to meet your parents."

"They won't bite. They're actually pretty nice people. You might like them."

She looked away. "I don't do parents very well. And Christmas…well, you know how I feel about that whole thing."

"Fine." He turned back to watch for the green light. It was dinner. No big deal. But if she had other plans, that wasn't any big deal, either.

"I didn't say I wouldn't go."

It was so ridiculous how this woman had him feeling like an adolescent. Hopeful one moment, annoyed as hell the next. He'd obviously missed the light change because someone behind them honked. So much for sitting through two lights. "We have two weeks. Just let me know."

"Listen, if you're going to be mad—"

"I'm not mad," he said calmly. "In fact, I have tickets for a concert Monday night if you'd like to go."

"Weird night for a concert." The wariness was back.

"It's not a ruse. I already showed you my etchings."

She didn't ask about the type of music or the group. Just smiled. "What time?"

"I can't remember. I'll have to give you a call. Don't forget to give me your cell number." He glanced over to see her reaction. Reluctance was written all over her face.

"Do you have a pen?"

He reached inside his jacket for one and handed it to her. "Or you can program your number into my cell."

She tried to hide a smile. "What if I don't like the concert? I might not go out with you again."

"Is that right?"

She nodded smugly, and wrote the number on a piece of torn paper.

"Here I thought you liked my fireplace."

"Oh, baby, I love your fireplace," she said, giving him the once-over.

"You're pretty hot yourself."

Liza laid her head back on the headrest and laughed softly. "It's easy being with you."

"I'm not sure how to take that."

She turned her head to face him, her cheek still pressed to the headrest. "This is touchy ground."

"Ah." Evan's gut tightened. Liza was one of those kind of unpredictable, free-spirited girls he'd known in high school. He'd always been attracted to them but never once dared asked one out. They would've laughed him back to the chemistry lab. "This is where you tell me I'm a nice guy and I'll make some woman a great husband one day."

"No, this is where I tell you that I think you're

a terrific guy and I love being with you and hope you don't run the other way."

Traffic was heavy and he had no business taking his eyes off the road, but he had to look over at her to see if she was teasing him. The earnestness in her eyes said otherwise. "Next time we'll have to get up early enough so I can make you breakfast."

She looked sad suddenly. "You cook?"

"A little."

"That's more than me."

"Good to know." He almost missed their exit. He had to do some fancy maneuvering to get over, and then waited until he cleared the off-ramp and said, "I know this Italian place with awesome baked ziti. We can go before the concert."

"What?" she asked, blinking at him, looking as if her thoughts were already miles away.

"Nothing," he said, and went back to concentrating on his driving with the feeling that she had no intention of joining him Monday evening.

LIZA PARKED AROUND the corner from the apartment complex. She'd stopped at a discount store and bought a new cream-colored sweater. Coming home in the same clothes she'd left wearing yesterday would be plain stupid. Overly paranoid maybe, but she wasn't taking any chances.

Her apartment key already in hand, she quietly made it up the stairs without incident. On the third-floor landing near Rick's apartment, a string of Christmas lights had been crushed and left on the concrete. It gave her a sick feeling and she made it the rest of the way with heavy steps.

Once inside, she dumped the package with her black sweater, along with her purse, on a kitchen chair. Just slightly bigger than a checkbook, the poor little brown leather purse was embarrassingly worn. Just like her shoes, her clothes and everything else she owned. Not totally true. She still had some nice things that she hadn't donated to charity, but were safely locked away in a small storage unit on the west side of town.

Mostly, though, she'd had to travel light. The more unstable Rick had grown, the more they'd had to move. God, how could it have been a year ago that she'd first walked off the set of *Just Between Us*. She was only supposed to have disappeared for a long weekend. Teach them all a lesson for taking her for granted. For shunning Rick.

She'd been bone-tired between partying too much with Rick and the demands of the show. It had really killed her that Eve and Jane hadn't liked him. They hadn't even been subtle about excluding him from social events. In retrospect, of course, they were right about him. But that they hadn't supported her decision had hurt. All she'd wanted was for them to be happy for her.

After she went to the bathroom and stared into the mirror—she was horrified at her gaunt appearance—she headed into the bedroom and flopped onto the bed. What did Evan see in her? She looked like hell. She didn't even have a job. He was probably one of those guys who liked rescuing women. Not that she needed his help. She could take care of herself. Because she'd done such a super bang-up job so far.

She closed her eyes. That one weekend a year ago had changed everything. She and Rick were supposed to have gone to Atlantic City for four days. Show Eve and Jane that she didn't need them, but they needed her. Atlantic City had been Rick's idea. He had this grand idea, he'd told her, and he had a surprise for her. Foolishly, she'd thought he was going to ask her to marry him.

What a joke. Poker and blackjack had proven to be his true loves. But he sucked at it. By the second day he'd drained her substantial checking account. When she'd refused to give up her savings, that's when he'd told her he had Eve's diaries.

Liza rolled over to bury her face in the pillow. She could see that scene in her head as if it happened an hour ago. They'd been sitting in the posh hotel suite he'd blithely paid for with her credit card. Him, so damn cocky, she wanted to tear his eyes out.

She'd totally panicked. She'd yelled and screamed and threatened to call the cops. He'd given her that evil smile she'd remember until the day she died, and told her that he was calling the shots from now on. If he couldn't get the money from her, he'd get it from the tabloids.

Eve's show had really taken off. She'd become the sweetheart of the local cable station with promises of bigger things to come. The truth was, her career could've weathered anything revealed in the diaries. The publicity might even have helped the show, which garnered its popularity partly from the frank, open discussions. But Eve, the woman, would have been deeply wounded by her private thoughts being splashed across the headlines. And Eve was Liza's friend, even more, the sister she never had.

The stupid bastard didn't care. Rick had been using smack right under Liza's nose, and she'd been too caught up in a maelstrom of lust and resentment to see what was happening. She'd totally underestimated him every step of the way. He'd even known about her inheritance before she had by intercepting the attorney's letter. When her savings was gone and she figured she finally had nothing more he wanted, he played his trump card.

The true irony was that now Liza saw that she hadn't loved Rick. Had she married him that weekend it would have been to defy Eve and Jane. Force them to accept him.

What a complete and utter moron she'd been. She was even crazier for replaying all this in her mind, which she did whenever she was exhausted. She doubted she'd had more than four hours sleep last night. Poor Evan. He didn't have the luxury of taking a nap, something in which she had every intention of indulging.

As her eyes drifted closed, just thinking of him made her smile. But only for a moment.

Because if she really wanted to be a stand-up person, she'd cut the cord with him. She didn't deserve a good man like Evan, and he didn't deserve her baggage.

RAIN POURED DOWN IN SHEETS. Visibility was almost nil. The road was so slick that cars skidded everywhere—through stop signs, into the middle of intersections. Sirens blared in the distance.

Damn stupid night to be riding a Harley. Rick used the back of his arm to wipe the rain from his face. He couldn't see shit. Couldn't even tell how close he was to the curb. Familiar with the intersection he was approaching, he knew there'd be a stop. He lightly applied the brakes. The bike wouldn't slow down. Panicked, he slammed down harder and went into a skid.

Light flashed off the side of the semi barreling toward him. The big white truck didn't stop. Rick veered to the left. He didn't see the massive oak tree. Until he wrapped his mangled body around it...

There were so many beautiful flowers. Oranges and yellows and stunning purples. Who the hell had sent them? How could anyone possibly have cared enough about his life or death? Liza watched them lower the casket into the ground and breathed a sigh of relief. She was finally rid of him. Finally. Thankfully...

Liza's eyes flew open. The dream hadn't woken her. Someone was knocking at the door. She closed her eyes again. If she ignored them, maybe they'd go away. Except if it were Rick. Her chest and gut tightened and she opened her eyes again. No, he'd be pounding. Screaming for her. But if she didn't stop the person who was out there now, they were likely to get his attention, too.

"I'll be right there," she called on her way to the bathroom. She stopped to splash her face with cold water. This was the second time she'd had the same dream. Both times it seemed so incredibly real. And both times she'd felt overwhelming relief. If that made her a horrible person, too bad.

That indifference didn't stop her hand from shaking as she peeked through the blind. Luckily, it was only Mary Ellen.

Liza opened the door, and covered an unexpected yawn.

"I wasn't sure you were home." Mary Ellen frowned. "I'm sorry. You were sleeping."

"Only a short nap." She pushed a hand through her messy hair. This afternoon she would splurge and get a trim and a manicure. She'd just paid the rent last week and had a few bucks left over. "Come in."

Mary Ellen hesitated. "Am I bothering you?"

Liza waved her inside. "Come on before Rick knows I'm home."

The woman quickly stepped inside. "I haven't seen him today."

Liza closed the door. "How about last night?"

"He was carrying on a bit. But someone from the

second floor threw a bottle at him and he disappeared."

"Have a seat." Liza went to the refrigerator, her entire body tensing. One of these days someone would call the police on him, and who knew how that would set him off. "I've got cola or orange juice."

"Juice, please."

"Where's Freedom?"

"Outside playing."

"No school today?" Liza asked casually, already knowing the answer. She really hated that Mary Ellen kept her out of school. The child was too gifted, for one thing, and in all of the craziness of Liza's childhood, education had been her saving grace. She'd been a good student in spite of herself, mostly because she'd loved books of any kind. They'd been her escape. And eventually, her fondness for reading helped get her into college.

"No," Mary Ellen said quietly, and took the glass Liza handed her.

Liza sat across from her with her own glass of juice. She didn't like the stuff but she'd taken her attorney's advice to heart. Showing up in court looking like crap wouldn't help the case. "She's a bright girl. I bet she does well in school."

Mary Ellen stared down at her lap. "I'm holding her out for a year."

"Is that wise?"

The woman's head came up. "Don't call social services. I teach her the best that I can at home."

"I know it's none of my business but—"

"You're leaving. What do you care?" The slight belligerence in Mary Ellen's voice was a total surprise. To her, too, apparently. She looked away sheepishly. "I'm sorry."

Liza didn't say anything at first. She had her own problems to deal with. "Look, in a couple of weeks I might be able to help you out. Get you a better apartment. Find a good school for Freedom."

Mary Ellen frowned. "Why would you want to do that?"

Good question. The old Liza wouldn't even have made friends with this woman in the first place. She sighed. "I might be coming into a little money."

Mary Ellen said nothing, but looked at her expectantly.

"And I want to be nice. That's all."

"Oh," she said, blinking several times, as if the concept was entirely foreign to her.

Liza got it. This was new for her, too. How self-absorbed she'd been these past few years. Hadn't she learned anything from her parents? Hadn't she sworn she'd never be like them? "Hey, when was the last time you got your hair cut?"

She fingered the ragged ends. "I cut mine and Freedom's hair last week."

"No, I mean going to an honest-to-goodness stylist who even washes and dries your hair for you."

Mary Ellen's eyebrows shot up. "That costs a lot of money."

"It's okay. We're going today. My treat."

"Really?"

"Yep. I know a place near the discount store around the corner that takes walk-ins."

"I'll have to take Freedom with us, but she can sit in a chair and wait."

"Good." Liza mentally calculated how much money she had in her purse and how much gas in her car. "We'll have burgers and shakes after that."

Mary Ellen beamed. "Cool. I'll go call Freedom."

"Not too loud, all right?"

Mary Ellen nodded, her solemn eyes acknowledging that if they woke up Rick, their afternoon would be ruined.

After the woman left, Liza went to brush her hair, and then got her purse and keys. Paying for two haircuts meant no manicure, but she didn't care. The look on Mary Ellen's face was worth it.

Liza made sure the door was locked and then went to meet the other two at Mary Ellen's end apartment. Freedom came running out the door.

"Mama's putting on lipstick," she said, all excited. "I never saw her do that before."

"Did she tell you why?"

"We're going out." She grinned, displaying a missing front tooth.

"Okay if I come?" Liza teased.

"If Rick will let you."

She stared in disbelief at the child. "I don't need Rick's permission."

She nodded, her expression somber. "Yes, you do. You're an abused woman just like Mama."

12

"MEET ME FOR LUNCH," Evan said the moment after Liza answered her cell phone.

She smiled. "Who is this?"

"The guy with the fireplace."

"Oh, that guy. In that case, I'm interested." She took the phone into the bedroom with her, and stretched out on the lumpy mattress. Just hearing his voice and her resolve to keep her distance went right out the window. "Are you at your office?"

"Yep. Someone canceled, so I have an extra half hour. Hold on a second."

She waited, listening to him talk to the nurse about referring a patient to an endocrinologist. She heard the rattle of paper near the phone, and then heard him murmuring some numbers as if reading from a chart. Finally, he gave the name of a couple of prescriptions for the nurse to call in to a pharmacy.

"Sorry about that," he said. "So what do you say? Want to save me from all this?"

Liza briefly closed her eyes. The moment she stepped foot out of the apartment Rick would be all over her. Like two days ago. What a nightmare. As soon as she'd gotten back with Mary Ellen and Freedom, he'd been in her face, demanding to know where she'd been and wanting money for cigarettes and booze. Of course, he was stoned out of his mind. And that Freedom had to witness any of it had made Liza so angry she'd nearly hauled off and knocked him down the stairs.

The worst of it had been the calm acceptance in Freedom's eyes. Liza had felt as low as an ant. She hadn't left the apartment since, and Freedom's words kept bouncing off the walls. The wise little girl knew what Liza had refused to face for the past year. The difficult thing was, what was she willing to do about it?

"What time?" she asked slowly.

"Give me another moment," he said, and she heard a woman's voice in the background.

"No problem," Liza said, but he was gone before she even got the words out.

She sat up briefly to rearrange the pillow behind her back and then settled in. She wasn't ready to leave right away, although at least her hair still looked decent. Amazing since all she'd done was lie around all day and feel sorry for herself.

She knew she had to have a serious talk with Evan, about the diaries, about Rick, and she dreaded it with every fiber of her being. It wasn't something she could comfortably explain over the phone, and she'd planned on doing it after the concert this evening. But maybe it was better to talk to him at lunch. Not only to get it over with, but a finite period of time would preempt questions she didn't want to answer.

The thing was, she wasn't quite sure what she wanted to say to him. Or at least how she wanted to say it. In less than two weeks her entire life would change, whether the judge ruled in her favor, or not. If she lost the suit...

She didn't want to think about that possibility. But her persistent avoidance was a huge problem, too. She had to be prepared for an adverse outcome. And getting seriously involved with Evan was exactly what she didn't need right now, for her own sanity, but mostly because it wasn't fair to him.

"Liza?"

"I'm here."

"Well, I'll have to rescind the lunch offer. One of my patients had the audacity to have an emergency."

"That's pretty rude of them."

"I thought so." Lowering his voice, he said, "But I plan on making it up to you tonight."

She smiled. "What's tonight?"

"The concert."

"Oh, I forgot."

"You are coming, aren't you?"

"Yes, I was teasing. What time?"

"I'll pick you up at your place at six-thirty. You'll have to give me the address."

Yeah, right. That would happen. "I'll meet you at the station parking lot."

"Come on, Liza. That's ridiculous."

Tonight she'd explain everything. Not now. "I thought you had a patient to attend to."

"She's on her way in. I have another ten minutes."

"Then grab something to eat."

"I'd rather talk to you," he said quietly. "I miss you."

A catch in her throat stopped her for a moment. "I saw you a day and a half ago."

"I know. It feels like a year."

"Stop it."

"Am I embarrassing you, or making you uncomfortable?" he asked, and she could hear the smile in his voice. "Too bad. I've gotten used to your mug across from me."

That couldn't possibly be true. Although why not? She missed him. As soon as she'd seen it was him calling, like a stupid twit, her pulse had quickened. "We haven't even gone out for two weeks yet."

"So?"

"That was eloquent."

He chuckled. "Deal with it."

Liza laughed. Even though lunch wasn't going to work out, she liked that he'd asked her. The afternoon wouldn't have finished in his bed. He apparently just wanted to talk. Share a meal. Because he missed her. Damn. This was not good. This was only supposed to be about sex.

"I'll have to be going," he said, "so about tonight…"

She squeezed her eyes shut and took a deep

breath, before staring at the cracked ceiling. "This will be the last time we meet at the station. I promise, Evan."

After a brief pause, he asked, "Is everything all right?"

At the quiet concern in his voice, her resolve to come clean with him seemed to strengthen. It felt so right that a year of tension seemed to evaporate from her body. She was going to tell him everything. No holding back. He'd be the only other person on this earth who knew about Rick and the diaries. She wouldn't ask for Evan's help. Wouldn't accept it if he offered. But no more lies. "The best it's been in a long time."

"Liza…"

"It's okay, really." She sat up. "Tonight. What shall I wear?"

"Something sexy."

"Right."

"Anything. You always look gorgeous. I'll see you at six-thirty."

"Hey, wait. I've been meaning to ask…" She wished she could see his face at that moment. She hoped she wasn't being totally nuts for hoping too much. "What do your folks usually have for Christmas dinner?"

LIZA HAD NEVER BEEN into clothes or fashion trends. When she'd worked for *Just Between Us* she'd actually owned a couple of dresses that she needed to wear on occasion. But even then, since her job was behind the scenes and had little to do with airtime, she mostly wore jeans. But tonight, she wanted to be different. She wanted to feel pretty. She really wanted to wow Evan.

How many times had she passed him in the hall at the station? How many times had she heard the assistant producers and wardrobe women making remarks about him? Every single one of them would've drooled all over themselves had he asked them out. In fact, she was pretty sure that Sally in wardrobe had taken the step herself. Although Liza didn't think anything came of it or she would've heard about it. The whole studio would've heard. Oh, boy, Evan would've loved that.

Liza smiled. Just because she'd thought of him. Man, when did she get so goofy? When had she started thinking beyond how great the sex was? She'd even told him she'd go to his parents with him for Christmas. The thought was sobering. She hadn't given her own mother a phone call for the past two Christmases. Nor had she received any calls from her.

It had been like that since Liza's father had died. Ironic since Liza had always thought he was the one who disrupted the cohesion of their family. But his body had barely gotten cold when resentment started to build, like a hurricane, gaining momentum each day and methodically destroying the fragile bond between Liza and her mother, until Liza couldn't stand the sight of the woman who was supposed to have protected her.

Restless suddenly, she paced the small apartment, trying to get mentally organized. If she wanted something nice to wear that meant shopping. Not her favorite thing but she could handle it. At least the outing would distract her from her decision to come clean. Since she'd hung up the phone she'd changed her mind twice. In less than two weeks everything would be decided. If she wanted to wait, she could explain everything to Evan then.

No, she was done being a coward. She liked Evan, and she wanted him to know the truth about Rick and about the lawsuit. He'd respect her more, right? Knowing that the lawsuit wasn't about personal gain. A huge plus, but most of all she didn't want to remain under Rick's thumb. She didn't want to be another Mary Ellen.

After Liza balanced her checkbook, trying not to get depressed, she wrote down a figure that she needed to sustain her and Rick for the month, and then another sum she'd be forced to give him for booze, drugs and cigarettes. The amount left was pitiful. No matter what the outcome of the lawsuit, she had to get a job after the first of the year. She looked forward to it. She never thought she'd actually long to be normal. Good grief, what had Evan done to her?

Shaking her head, she grabbed her car keys and purse. She had three hours to get to the bank, go shopping and deal with Rick. This afternoon she'd give him an extra forty bucks. That ought to get him good and stoned. And out of her hair for the evening. Yeah, that was mean and ugly, and she didn't care. As long as he stayed out of her face.

HER COAT WAS OLD and ratty and should've been retired a year ago but Liza slipped it on anyway and quietly left the apartment. She didn't want anyone to see her dressed in the new off-the-shoulder royal-blue sweater and sleek black pants, not even Mary Ellen, and least of all Rick. Although she was pretty sure she didn't have to worry about him. He was already so damn wasted before she gave him the vodka he'd asked her to pick up earlier.

She knew, too, that he had two extra grams of smack stashed under the couch. In the old days she would've confiscated it in the hope he'd forget about it. That maybe if a day without the stuff stretched into a week his craving would diminish and the old Rick would be back. She'd been incredibly naive to think she could stop him from getting high by throwing out his drugs and booze. He always found more. Always. As if by magic. Even when it seemed impossible.

Just like her father had seemed to always have money for his beer and gin, when only canned tomato soup stocked the pantry for his wife and child, or that for a week at a time she'd been sent to school without lunch money, or even a lousy piece of fruit to quiet her empty belly.

Now she knew better. She couldn't change someone who didn't want to change themselves.

All she could do was maintain her physical and emotional distance to keep herself as sane as possible.

Once she made it to her car, she removed the coat and threw it on the backseat before she got in. For a second she thought she heard the revving of a motorcycle engine and she quickly looked around. A few cars were parked behind her, and two kids were playing with a large orange ball. No motorcycles in sight.

Chalking it up to nerves, she started the car. Traffic was fine on this neighborhood side street, but she knew it would be heavy on the way to Midtown so she allowed herself an extra ten minutes. She'd been lucky to find the sweater on sale. It was truly gorgeous, and it fit her perfectly. So did the satiny slacks, and it felt as if she were in high school again, so anxious to see Evan that she wanted to burst.

She wasn't the most patient driver, especially during rush hour, and a dozen expletives later she pulled into the station's parking lot. A whole lot more cars than normal were still there and she wondered what was going on. Did the unusual crowd have anything to do with *Just Between Us*? Sometimes they had a special show or a special guest. And as senior producer, had she still been working there, that show would have been her baby.

A pang of nostalgia got her right where it smarted the most, and she had to block it as fiercely as a mother bear protecting her cub. She had to stay sharp. Unemotional. Tonight was important.

She found a spot at the far end of the parking lot. No way would Evan be able to see her, which meant she had to get out and wait closer to the station door. The idea certainly didn't thrill her. She didn't need to bump into Eve or Jane or any of the other lottery winners. But she had little choice, short of parking illegally, which in itself was nearly impossible in the crowded lot.

After checking her makeup in the rearview mirror, she climbed out of the car. Out of habit, she glanced around, although she'd bet her car that Rick wouldn't wake up until tomorrow. Another check of her watch and then she started in the direction of the station door.

Evan was already standing outside. Instead of a sports coat, he wore a gray suit and red tie, which made her glad she'd gotten more dressed up than usual. He smiled as soon as he saw her, and her heart all but burst in her chest. A large pickup truck blocked their views for a moment and then she stepped around it just as he came off the curb.

He pointed toward his car, which was parked in the middle of the third row. She nodded and veered off in that direction. He caught up with her partway there and surprised her with a kiss on the lips and a hug that stole her breath.

"Hi to you, too," she said, taking a step back.

"You look fantastic."

She scoffed, plucking at the top of her sweater, and with a pronounced Southern accent, said, "This old thing."

They both laughed, and he slipped an arm around her shoulders, steering them on course. "Of course, you look pretty damn good in jeans, too."

"Someone's looking to get lucky tonight."

Smiling, he hugged her closer. "I already am lucky."

"Corny, Gann, very corny."

He laughed, and she felt the vibration in his chest. A combination of muskiness and confidence, his familiar scent filled her with a deep contentment that was both foreign and scary, yet she wouldn't trade it for anything. Having his arm around her, pressing against the strength of his chest…well, that made her feel invincible. Foolish, yes. She didn't care. Not even the tiniest bit.

The air was a little chilly and she slid her arm around his waist. He glanced down at her and kissed her temple. She heard laughter behind them and turned to see where it was coming from. A group of people were exiting the building.

"A Christmas party, I think," Evan said.

"For *Just Between Us*?"

He shook his head. "The studio next door. I overheard a cameraman talking about it when I was getting coffee."

"That's one point for not working. No Christmas parties and baby showers you have to go to."

"Scrooge."

"Guilty and without apology." Until she spotted Eve's car, Liza hadn't even thought about looking to see if Eve or Jane's cars were still there. She took another look over her shoulder. She still hadn't quite shaken the feeling that someone was watching her, but paranoia was nothing new.

"What's wrong?" Evan stopped and turned around, too.

"Nothing. I saw Eve's car. I thought maybe— Come on. I'm hungry. I hope you're feeding me before the concert." She tugged him along with her toward his Camry. "I never asked you what kind of concert it is."

"My nephew's third-grade class is putting on a Christmas pageant."

She looked at him. "I hope you're kidding."

"I don't have a nephew."

She pinched his arm.

"Ouch." Evan chuckled. "I wish I did have one, then maybe Mom would back off on the 'I should be a grandmother already' thing."

"That's right. You're the oldest."

"You're an only child. You must get it worse."

"Hardly."

"Really?"

"My mother could barely cope the first time around. Grandmother material she isn't."

"But your dad was—" Evan frowned at her, and she truly wished she'd kept her mouth shut. "Who took care of you?"

"Me. Didn't do too bad a job, huh?" She nudged him with her shoulder. "Come on. Lighten up."

But it was too late. The pensive frown that

caused lines between his dark eyebrows had grown deeper, but thankfully there was no pity in his face or she wouldn't have been able to stand it. She didn't dwell on what her parents should or shouldn't have done. She'd made peace with the past. Made peace with the fact that she and her mother could never have a relationship.

They reached his car and in true Evan fashion, he walked her all the way around to the passenger side and opened her door. She didn't argue. In fact, in a tiny, tiny way, she was beginning to like it. Not that she'd admit it in a thousand years.

She smiled and was about to get in when he stopped her. He tilted her chin up and kissed her. Not a brief friendly kiss, but one that told anyone who happened to be watching that this was no casual relationship. His tongue teased the seam of her lips and she opened up to him more out of shock than anything. When he finally withdrew, she had the urge to look around and make sure no one saw the display.

Instead, she slid onto the seat and let him close the door. While she waited for him to join her inside the car, she noticed a couple staring at Evan as he went around the hood. The rumors would start flying around the station tomorrow. Glad she wasn't…

The passenger door flew open. Startled, she swung around and met Rick's furious bloodshot blue eyes. Oh, no.

"Get out, you stupid lying bitch."

"What are you doing here?" She looked back toward Evan. He'd just climbed behind the wheel.

She glared at Rick, fear clogging her throat. "Get away from me. Get the hell away," she spat out.

"Liza, what's happening?"

She couldn't look at Evan now. She kept her gaze on Rick, struggling not to let him see her fear. "Leave right now, or I swear you won't see another penny."

"We've come too far, baby." He reached for her, and she slapped his face. Momentarily he moved back.

Cursing, Evan got out of the car.

"Evan, no. Please." She couldn't stop him, so she pushed Rick out of the way and got out, too.

Evan was coming around the hood. People walking to their cars stopped to watch the commotion. She couldn't let this play out, not in front of all these people, especially not in front of Evan.

She put up a restraining hand. "Evan, please. It's okay. I can handle this."

His face was dark with fury. Focused on Rick, he wouldn't even look at her. "Step away from the lady."

"Lady?" Rick laughed.

"Stop it!" Liza grabbed Rick's arm. "Let's go." He wouldn't budge. He wouldn't break eye contact with Evan. Desperate, she whispered in his ear, "Let's leave right now, and tonight will be like old times."

He blinked, and then his gaze darted to her. "Okay, baby, whatever you say." And then, shooting a triumphant look at Evan, he snaked an arm around her waist and put his filthy mouth on hers.

She wanted to jerk away. Her stomach rolled at his touch, at the foulness of his breath. But she couldn't without making matters worse. She knew Rick too well, and to make this all stop, she could only give in, pretend she wanted the kiss.

Finally, she tugged Rick away, and tried not to look at Evan, but she couldn't help herself. At the last moment, she slid him a glance. The shocked hurt on his face cut her to the bone.

13

EVAN STOOD PERFECTLY STILL, watching her weave through the cars, holding hands with that filthy sleaze, until she was out of sight. He couldn't move if he tried. He could barely breathe.

She'd sworn that Rick was out of the picture, and Evan had believed her. It wasn't just that she'd lied, but the sight of Rick himself was hard to take. The long, shaggy, dirty hair and filthy jeans. He couldn't bear to imagine what was under the black leather jacket. Evan hadn't even gotten that close and he could smell the guy from fifteen feet away.

And Liza had kissed him. The unbidden image sent a shiver down Evan's spine. How could she have done that? And in front of him? What hold did this guy have on her? Or hadn't she thought Evan could've handled that poor excuse for a man? Is that why she'd gone off with him? She hadn't wanted to leave with him, Evan could tell that much. But why not call the police? None of this made sense. Liza was too strong a woman to allow herself to be treated like that.

He drew in an unsteady breath. What a chump he'd been. He'd actually broken his own damn rule and started to have feelings for her. Although he couldn't complain. They'd openly agreed their relationship was just about sex. So that was on him.

"Evan?"

It took a moment to register that someone was talking to him. He turned around. Decked out in cocktail dresses, Eve Best and another woman he'd seen around the station stood a few feet away. The shaken looks on their faces told him they'd seen everything.

Damn.

"Yeah?" he said, realizing he still stood in front of his car. He patted his pocket for the keys and then remembered they were already in the ignition.

"Evan, can we talk for a moment?" Eve followed him to the driver's door.

"We did that the other day."

"I know." She got in the way when he reached for the door handle. "I wasn't helpful. I've felt badly ever since."

"Well, I'm not feeling so hot myself right now, so if you'll excuse me…"

"Please, Evan." Eve wouldn't back off, and there was no way he could open the door without ramming her. "Do you know Jane?" she asked, indicating the blond woman with serious blue eyes beside her. "She's with *Just Between Us*."

Evan nodded to her, and she gave him a small smile.

"I suppose you figured out that was Rick," Eve said.

Evan's laugh was bitter. "Uh-huh, I kind of figured that out."

"I was excited to hear that you were seeing Liza." Jane glanced at Eve. "We both were. We thought that meant Rick wasn't around."

"We hoped that Liza had come to her senses, and would come back to the show," Eve said.

"Come back to us," Jane added softly.

"Hmm, it doesn't appear that's the case. Look, ladies, I have a concert to—"

"Do you care about her?" Jane asked with a sad earnestness that was difficult to blow off.

"I did. Or at least I thought I did."

"It's Rick. It's not her."

"You know Liza better than I do," he said, aware that people lingered within earshot. "Does she strike you as a woman who'd put up with a man she didn't want?"

"But Rick is—" they both said at the same time, and then stopped and looked at each other.

Eve spoke next. "The three of us have been friends since we were eleven. I had just lost both of my parents in a car accident when I met Liza. My life had been turned upside down. I was horribly unhappy." She glanced at Jane. "She was going through her own preteen angst. And then Liza came into our lives. And she was fun and mischievous and got us into all kinds of trouble. But she always pulled us back out."

"Always," Jane said, nodding. "We were like the Three Musketeers, you know? Always together.

Always backing each other up. In high school I was really self-conscious about wearing braces, and if a kid even looked at me wrong Liza was in their face."

Evan frowned. Nice trip down memory lane. What did it have to do with him?

"We went to college together. We started this damn show together," Eve continued, motioning toward the station, the frustration evident in her stormy eyes. "Nothing ever came between us."

"Except Rick," Jane finished.

"We didn't help matters by telling her what a bum he was. But she should've known better. Running off with him like that was—" Eve gave an impatient shake of her head. "He's behind this lawsuit. I just know it."

Evan put up a hand. "That's none of my business. At this point, I really don't give a damn what she's doing, or why she's doing it."

"I don't care about the lawsuit or the money," Eve said with a sincerity that gave him pause. "She's a really good person, but you already know that or else you wouldn't have gone out with her. We're simply asking that you not judge her too harshly."

"Don't give up on her." Jane laid a hand on his arm. "Please."

He stared at the two women, not knowing what to think. How could they defend her? How could they possibly give a damn about her? At one point she obviously had been very special to them, which made her betrayal all the more devastating and incomprehensible.

But yet here they were, pleading her case. What the devil did they expect him to do about it, anyway? She went willingly with Rick, disgusting sort that he was. Granted, Liza probably hadn't wanted to cause a scene, but to kiss the guy like that? Evan got queasy at the thought. Inexcusable. He'd already endured one cheating, lying woman. That was one too many in a lifetime.

"I really do have a concert to attend," he said, and waited for Eve to step away from the door.

She nodded and moved back with a tight slant to her lips. He didn't even want to look at Jane. That one wore her heart in full view. Not that either of them could sway him. He'd had more than enough of Liza Skinner.

"Who the fuck was that guy?" Rick's words had started to slur a block away from the station. Whatever he'd taken earlier obviously started to kick in.

Good thing she'd insisted on driving despite his ranting about leaving his bike behind. "Nobody."

"Nobody." He snorted and reached over, fisting a handful of her sweater. "You dressed like this for nobody."

"Get your goddamn hands off me."

He made a grab for the steering wheel. She shoved him away but momentarily lost control and the car swerved erratically over the center line. Horns blared, a jogger yelled, but luckily the oncoming traffic was far enough away that everyone escaped damage.

"Do that again and I'll drive you straight to the police station." Her hands shook so hard that she gripped the wheel until her knuckles turned white.

When he didn't answer, she slid a look at him. His head drooped, his chin nearly touching his chest, and he appeared to be struggling to keep his eyes open.

She took a deep breath and said nothing more for the rest of the ride home. He stayed quiet, too, his breathing deep and even, and after she parked the car she slowly opened her door, hoping he'd stay asleep. She had no qualms about leaving him out here. Maybe she'd get lucky and he'd freeze to death. The stupid bastard.

Using the back of her arm, she wiped her mouth. It didn't help. Rick's revolting taste had crawled down her throat, permeated her belly so that she wanted to puke. She could feel him in her hair, smell him in the fabric of her new sweater. She couldn't wait to take it off. Throw it into one of the giant garbage bins behind the complex. No, burn it. Even better.

She closed her eyes and prayed Rick would stay asleep. If he did, she could call Evan and explain...she choked back a sob. Explain what? What could she possibly tell him that would erase the past half hour?

God, she would never, ever, not in a million years forget the wounded look on Evan's face as she walked away. Rick's disgusting arm around her. The bleakness in Evan's eyes was enough to want to make her want to weep. How could she have been so foolish? She'd underestimated Rick before, and swore she never would again. Now she wasn't the only one paying for her stupidity.

Liza got out of the car and was just about to close the door when he stirred. She froze, hoping it would turn out to be nothing. He muttered an oath and brought his head up. He looked straight at her, the streetlight shining in his haggard face.

Sadness swept over her. He'd been good-looking and charming once, but smack and booze had dragged him through the gutter a couple of times. He looked fifty, yet he wouldn't be thirty until next month. Another wasted life.

His head came up. "What are you looking at?" Spit flew everywhere. Some of it had dried at the corners of his mouth. Some of it caked to his white T-shirt where the leather jacket didn't cover.

She shuddered. "We're home."

He squinted, looking around as if he thought she was trying to trick him.

For an instant, she'd actually experienced a pang of sympathy. Amazing. She slammed the door and started toward their building. Screw him. She didn't care that the car would be unlocked overnight. Right now she didn't care about anything. Tomorrow her attorney could tell her she'd been awarded a hundred million dollars and it would mean nothing. After what she'd just done to Evan, she didn't deserve the clothes on her back.

She heard Rick get out of the car, and she mentally braced herself for what was inevitably ahead for the evening. When he yelled for her to stop, she kept walking. It was the dinner hour and the complex was quiet, but it didn't matter if he made a scene here. Not like it had mattered back at the station parking lot. In front of Evan. Eve and Jane had been there, too. She'd caught sight of them out of the corner of her eye as she was leaving.

Sniffling, she picked up her pace when she sensed him behind her. Any vile thing he had to say to her could wait until they got inside. She got to the stairs and ran up to the second landing before she turned around to check his progress.

He staggered quite far behind, using parked cars for support, taking two steps and falling back one. If he couldn't make it up the stairs, that was his tough luck. She'd leave him where he was and hide out until he slept off whatever crap he'd stuffed into his system.

She headed up the next flight of stairs, making it halfway up when she heard a car alarm go off. Several apartment doors opened and people stuck their heads out. She didn't turn around. She knew what had set off the alarm. Rick had gotten too close to one of those new cars with a touchy system. The blaring lasted just long enough to be annoying. Maybe he'd get his butt kicked by one of the bikers who lived on the second floor. Wouldn't hurt her feelings.

Finally, she got to her floor and couldn't help

sneaking another look. Rick stumbled to the bottom of the stairs. He plopped down on the first step. She continued to her apartment, barely getting the door unlocked when she heard him yell something about not being finished with her.

She went inside, closed the door and leaned back against it. What a nightmare. What a friggn' nightmare. Less than two weeks and it would've been over. What had she done so wrong in her life that she deserved this kind of karma? She heard him yell again, and slowly garnered her mistake.

She was prolonging the nightmare. If she got him to his apartment, he'd pass out soon and she'd be in peace for the rest of the night. Yeah, that's what she'd thought before she'd left to meet Evan. Shit. She couldn't think about him right now, she told herself as she hurried from the apartment. She had to gather her strength. Get Rick inside. He couldn't possibly stay awake much longer. Tomorrow he'd have questions, and she'd have lies.

He was so out of it by the time she got downstairs she was afraid she wouldn't be able to get him to the third floor. But as soon as he saw her, the point was moot. He seemed to rally. Mumbling curses, he grabbed the railing and pulled himself upright.

"You trying to sneak away from me again," he spat out, his anger sending him backward. He hooked his arm around the railing in time to keep himself from falling.

"I'm trying to help you," she said tightly and

started to reach for his arm. The thought of touching him gave her the willies and she immediately withdrew. "Can you make it up the stairs?"

"I made it down, didn't I?" He stared at her with so much hatred it shrouded her like a dark cloud.

For a moment she flashed on an image of her father, looming over her, his hand drawn back. Although he'd rarely hit her, the threat had been enough.

She blinked. Her father was gone. But with a shudder, she realized she'd replaced him with Rick.

He wobbled, leaning toward her. "Get out of my way."

She put her hands up. "Fine."

She stood back and watched him struggle to the next step. Even with all the crap he'd put her through, there were times—like back at the car—when she'd actually felt sorry for him. When she'd truly wished she knew how to help him fight the addiction. Right now, he could fall and break his neck and she wouldn't shed a single tear.

Unable to watch him another moment, she fled up the stairs but stayed on the second-floor landing. She waited until he got close, and then she went to the third floor. He crawled up to the last landing. Watching him, she was amazed how she could feel nothing. No pity. No anger. Nothing.

He'd left his apartment unlocked, surprising because he was usually worried about his drug stash. She pushed the door open and waited for him to approach before stepping aside. His foul breath reached her before he did. She turned her face before she gagged.

"What are you doing standing out here?" He fell against her, and she automatically grabbed his arm and shoved him away. "You didn't forget your promise, huh, Liza?"

She reared her head back. How could he remember that? Not that she had any intention of spending the night anywhere near him. "Get inside."

He could barely lift his lids. "You first."

"Come on, Rick."

"You want the diaries? Get your ass in there."

She stood her ground for a moment, and then realized how stupid she was being. The important thing was to get him inside. He wouldn't last long on his feet.

"Fine." She went first, stepping over empty bottles and the same fast-food wrappers that had been there for two weeks. The place smelled as bad as he did.

He slammed the door behind him and then kicked an empty tumbler out of his way. It hit the coffee table and shattered, pieces of glass flying across the carpet.

She stepped farther back, giving him a wide berth to the couch. But he headed for her instead. Panic gripped her. He was in too bad a condition to be a serious physical threat, but that didn't mean he couldn't do damage. Besides, just the thought of him touching her again…

"Where's the rest of my stash?" Rick asked.

"What are you talking about?"

"You have it."

She drew in a deep breath. They'd gone through this before, but that was when she'd thought she was helping by hiding his stuff. "I don't have anything of yours. You must have hidden it and forgot where you put it."

He grunted in disbelief, but then he blinked, looking confused. "You don't have it?"

"No."

He looked toward the kitchen, and then stumbled in that direction, muttering to himself.

She heard the oven door open and then the rattle of paper.

Rick reappeared with a bag in his hand. He went straight for the couch, without looking at her, and went to work preparing his injection as if he'd forgotten she was there.

Liza didn't move, in fact she barely breathed as she watched him prepare for his trip into oblivion. With what he'd already ingested, in the next few minutes, he'd be out and she'd be home free.

He took a rattling breath, and then slumped against the paisley upholstered pillows, his eyes closed. She turned slowly toward the door. Keeping her gaze on him, she moved as quietly as possible. She stepped on something that crackled, and she froze until she was certain he hadn't been disturbed. After transferring her attention to the floor in front of her, she continued toward the door.

She grabbed hold of the doorknob.

The next second his hand circled her wrist. She cried out, more surprised than hurt, and twisted free. He stumbled, too weak and wasted to maintain a grip. But still, he swiped at the air, trying to strike her. She shoved him hard, and watched him trip over a bottle.

He hit the floor, butt first, and then his head slammed the corner of the coffee table. He lay there, not moving, his legs askew, his eyes closed, his ravaged face a deadly pallor.

She covered her mouth, cutting off a frightened cry. Jesus, had she killed him? She lowered her hand from her mouth. "Rick?" No answer. No movement. Not even a twinge. She walked over to him and dropped to her knees. "Rick!"

Nothing.

Silence. Deafening silence.

Her hands shook so badly that when she checked his wrist she knew that she wouldn't find a pulse even if there was one. She stared hard at the side of his neck, looking for a pulse there. Her vision blurred. She tried to swallow but her mouth was too dry. She pulled back, sinking onto her heels, and wrapped her arms around herself. Her upper arms were tender, bruised from his grip earlier.

How many times had she wished him dead? She'd even dreamed about it. What had she done? She tried to take a deep breath but it wouldn't come. She closed her eyes and forced herself to breathe. She tried a visualization technique she'd learned in college, but as soon as she summoned the image of

Eve and Jane and herself playing on the beach in Fort Lauderdale the summer after they'd all met, panic overtook her.

She opened her eyes. The diaries. If he died, would she ever find them? Could they still hurt Eve?

She had to calm down. If he died, she'd have more than that to worry about. Everyone would think she'd killed him on purpose. No one would blame her, not here in the complex, anyway. They all thought Rick was an asshole. But that gave her motive.

"Oh, Rick, you stupid bastard." She hugged herself tighter, rocking back and forth. She freed her arms and shook out her hands. She had to find a pulse. If not, she'd have to call 911.

The thought terrified her. She picked up his cold, limp hand and pressed her thumb to his wrist. Was that a pulse? Did she feel something? Or did she want it so badly she imagined it?

She sat back again, staring at his lifeless body. There was no blood. That was good. She took her first really deep breath. Maybe this had nothing to do with the fall. The amount of drugs and booze in his system could be enough to take him down.

"Come on, Liza, think," she said out loud. She could call Mary Ellen to at least help her find a pulse.... No, the woman had enough trouble of her own. If the police ended up getting involved...

Evan.

He was a doctor. He would know what to do.

She scrambled to her feet, while looking for her purse. She saw it laying on the floor by the door. Quietly she got back down and crawled toward it, and then glanced over her shoulder, before getting out her cell phone. She pressed his speed dial number. "Evan? Please, Evan. I need your help."

14

HE ALMOST HADN'T answered the phone. He usually didn't when he was driving. The pager was a different matter. Only his nurse and answering service had that number, so a call usually meant a patient emergency.

"Evan?"

"Liza?" He wasn't sure. Her voice barely made it to a whisper.

"I need your help. I think I—" Her voice cracked and she sniffled. "Please come."

"Where?"

"My apartment."

He nearly missed a stop sign. He pulled over to the shoulder. "What's going on?"

"I can't explain over the phone. Please, Evan, please… I need you."

Pitifully, that's all it took. He got her address, listened as calmly as he could as she gave directions, because she was anything but calm, and then he turned the car around. He did hope he wasn't being a damn fool. She'd said she needed him, and he went running. Barely a question asked.

In his defense, she did sound panicked. Even though she hadn't explained the problem, it had to be about Rick. If he'd hurt her... Evan couldn't think about that. He couldn't think about the conversation with Eve and Jane that he'd kept replaying in his head. He needed to concentrate on his driving. Traffic was heavy and he wasn't that familiar with the area where she lived.

Half an hour and two wrong turns later, he saw the name of the apartment complex she'd given him. He had to look twice because several letters were missing from the sign. After he entered the parking lot, he understood how big the complex was, with no particular method to the layout. Reluctantly, he stopped to ask a man in a gray hoodie getting groceries out of the trunk of a car where to find building three. But the man didn't speak English.

The place was in disgraceful shape, with litter on the ground next to the trash cans, and damaging potholes throughout the parking lot. The buildings were no better, with improper outside lighting and chunks of missing railing going up the stairs. Broken bottles littered the ground. This couldn't be right.

He stopped the car and studied the directions he'd written down. How could Liza live in a dump like this? Aesthetics aside, the place wasn't safe, especially not for a single woman. But his directions were right on. All he needed was to find building three.

After taking the next turn, he saw a chipped number against the dirty brick that could either be three or eight. Then he saw Liza's car parked near the building. There were no empty spaces nearby but he managed to squeeze into an illegal spot near the stairs. If he got a ticket, so be it. He needed to get to Liza.

As soon as he got out of the car, she stepped out of the shadows near the stairs. No coat, even though it had gotten terribly cold since sunset, and still wearing the off-the-shoulder blue sweater she had on earlier. She didn't come to him, but stayed where she was, shivering, hugging herself.

"Liza, are you okay?" he asked, quickly looking her over as he hurried toward her.

She shook her head.

He got to her but carefully kept his hands to himself. "Are you injured?"

She shook her head again, her eyes frightened, her face pale.

"Okay, good." He wanted to reach for her, hold her against his chest but he kept his hands to himself.

"Come," she whispered, her voice catching.

She turned around and led him up the stairs, one hand clinging to the rail. She faltered once, and he bracketed her waist with his hands until she steadied herself, and then let go when she continued.

She got to the third floor and went only a few steps before stopping in front of an apartment to wait for him.

"Is this your apartment?" he asked. She said nothing but just stood there shivering.

"No. Rick's. That's mine," she said, glancing over her shoulder.

A bad feeling gripped Evan's gut and wouldn't let go. "Is Rick hurt?"

Her lips quivered. She opened her mouth but nothing came out. With a soft cry she launched herself against him and wrapped her arms around his waist, clinging to him as if she teetered on the edge of a precipice and letting go would mean certain death.

"I think I killed him," she whispered. "He's not breathing."

Christ Almighty. He gently pushed her back and looked at her terrified face. What the hell had she done? "What happened?"

"I shoved him. He hit his head on the corner of the table."

"You have a key?"

"It's unlocked."

He turned the knob and the door opened. Among the litter, Rick laid on the dingy carpet, one leg twisted ominously, his face pasty white.

"Did you call 911?" Evan went to the man and crouched beside him.

"No. Just you."

He looked sharply at her. "Do it. Now."

She hesitated. "I didn't mean it. He lunged for me, and I shoved him…."

"Liza, please," Evan said calmly. "Make the call."

She didn't move. Just stood there staring at the

shaggy-haired man on the floor, as if she were in a trance, her entire body shaking.

"Liza."

She nodded and, with trembling hands, pulled her cell phone out of her pocket.

He checked the pulse at Rick's neck. Faint but steady. Evan breathed in with relief. The pulse was weak enough he could see how she'd missed it, but it was there. The guy was definitely alive. Gingerly, Evan slid his hands under Rick's head. No blood or obvious wounds. His arms and legs seemed all right, too. He checked his eyes. Not good.

"It's my fault," Liza said, staring. "He was already high and I should've stopped him from shooting up. But I didn't. I wanted him to shut up. To go to sleep so I could call you and explain. I wanted him dead." She shot Evan a panicked look, as if realizing her admission.

Evan forced himself to stay focused on his patient. He had a lot of questions for her, but now wasn't the time. "Did you call 911?"

"Yes." Tears streamed down her face. She seemed to be having difficulty drawing a breath. "What have I done?"

"He's not dead."

She blinked. Disappointment flashed across her face. She quickly lost it. Relief took its place, but was it real?

The hair on the back of Evan's neck stood. He definitely hadn't mistaken the disappointment. The thought of it made him queasy. Was she using him to help mount her defense? Had she wanted to get rid of Rick that badly that she'd tried to kill him? He did not want to believe that. "Do you know if he might have used anything else besides the heroin?"

"He's been drinking a lot. Beer and vodka mostly."

"Did you give him the drugs?"

She visibly swallowed. "I gave him the money to buy them."

Evan looked away from her and stared down at Rick. "Why did you call me?"

"You're a doctor."

"The paramedics would've gotten here faster," he said, meeting her eyes.

"I was scared, Evan. I didn't know what to do. I thought I'd killed a man."

He looked back down at Rick. She might not be directly responsible, but the guy was in bad shape. Would he make it? Evan had no idea.

"You're angry." She dropped down beside him, putting a hand on his thigh for balance.

"I'm confused."

"I'll tell you everything." She looked around at the first sound of the sirens. "I was going to tell you tonight at dinner."

Of course she was. "Right now, let's concentrate on getting Rick to a hospital."

"I swear, Evan," she whispered, desperation making her voice thick. "I know you don't believe me but—"

He picked her hand up and set it aside, and then got to his feet. Had this been her plan all along? Get rid of her boyfriend and use Evan to justify a self-defense claim? He really didn't know what to think at this point. Maybe it was better that he didn't think. Go on autopilot. Be Dr. Gann and get Rick taken care of before engaging in any conversations with Liza.

"Where are you going?" she asked.

He was at the door already. "To flag down the paramedics. This building isn't easy to find."

"I'm sorry, Evan. I didn't know what to do. I really didn't mean to get you involved."

He stopped and looked at her, crumpled in a heap on the floor. In spite of himself, he softened. He had to at least give her the benefit of the doubt. But that didn't mean he'd let himself be her doormat. "I have no intention of getting involved."

LIZA HAD NEVER FELT so alone in her entire life. Ironic, since just yesterday she'd dared to be happy, to actually harbor hope in her heart that Evan would be someone with whom she could share a part of herself. But it wasn't his fault that everything had fallen apart. She screwed up. In a major way. Would he ever forgive her?

She looked over at Rick, his mouth partially open, disgusting spittle caked at the corners. She shouldn't hate him. He deserved her sympathy. But she did hate him. More than she'd hated anyone. Even her father.

The sound of the sirens got so loud that the ambulance had to be right outside. She struggled to her feet and went to the door but stayed inside. She didn't want to see any of her neighbors, and they'd all be out there, gawking, wondering if the ambulance had come for her or Rick.

Nearly everyone had heard Rick's vitriolic rantings at one time or another. They'd seen her trying to sneak off, and heard him yelling at the top of his lungs to get her ass back to the apartment. Stoned out of his mind, Rick had knocked on doors in the middle of the night looking for her. If he didn't make it, what would those people tell the police?

She hoped Mary Ellen and Freedom weren't out there, too. But then why wouldn't they be? The sirens were so damn loud....

Liza put a hand to her throbbing head and ducked for a quick look. The paramedics had just pulled their equipment from the back of the van. Evan said something to one of them. The man nodded and got inside the ambulance, a minute later climbing out and dragging the end of a gurney. The second paramedic grabbed the other end and they brought it up the stairs, swiftly and efficiently, followed by Evan.

She got out of the way, and they entered the apartment and immediately went to work on Rick. Liza stepped farther back, unable to stop shaking. Yes, she still felt horrible and responsible for Rick lying there, but watching Evan made her feel worse. He was such a good man. Always doing the right thing, and she totally didn't deserve him. Not that it mattered either way now.

She really wanted to talk to him, though. Even if she never saw him again, she wanted him to know the truth about Rick, the lawsuit, everything. It would kill her if Evan thought she'd betrayed him. But it wasn't going to be easy to talk to him when he wouldn't even meet her eyes.

Time seemed to inch by as she waited, expecting to see the police show up at the door. But the only people she saw were nosy neighbors ducking their heads in for a look. Evan made them move as the paramedics prepared Rick for transport. Once the path was clear, they picked Rick up and started down the stairs.

Neither paramedic said a word to her, and she knew she had Evan to thank for that. Not that she thought she'd get out of being questioned, but later she'd be more composed. She grabbed her purse, making sure her keys hadn't fallen out, and then followed them down, face straight ahead so that she didn't have to look at the crowd of people who'd gathered. Not trusting her weakened knees, she kept a firm hold on the railing, even when she heard Freedom call out to her.

But Liza did look up then, and motioned Freedom to stay back. Mary Ellen stared in horrified silence. Liza managed to give her a reassuring smile before joining Evan and the paramedics at the back of the ambulance.

"We're taking him to Grady Memorial," the

taller, muscled paramedic said, with a glance in her direction.

"I guess I should follow," she said, not sure if the words had stayed in her head or passed her lips.

Evan looked at her, his gaze going to her trembling hands, which she still couldn't seem to control. "I'll take you."

"Thank you," she said softly.

"Go get in the car." He pointed the remote at the Camry and unlocked the doors. "I'll be right there."

She nodded, her gaze straying to the ambulance. The doors were open and she could see Rick lying on the gurney. One of the paramedics was hooking him up to something.

"Go, Liza."

She looked over at Evan, wanting reassurance. His expression was grim.

EVAN SPOKE TO the E.R. doctor for a few minutes, giving him a rundown on Rick's condition and the events leading up to his losing consciousness. He probably should've let Liza do the talking, but she was still a mess and since he was pretty sure she had nothing to do with what happened to Rick, Evan didn't see the point.

He went to the crowded waiting area where he told her he'd meet her. She sat forward in one of the hard brown chairs, hands clasped, her elbows resting on her thighs, her head hanging. She didn't seem to be shaking too much anymore. Good. He wouldn't have to give her a sedative.

She glanced up when he picked up her purse, which had been sitting on the chair next to her. "How's he doing?"

He handed her the purse, and then sat down. "He'll live."

This time she genuinely looked relieved. Straightening, she asked, "Was it the drugs?"

Evan nodded. "I'm pretty sure he has a concussion, too, but the drugs are what got him."

"Are the police coming?"

"You didn't do anything wrong, Liza."

She briefly closed her eyes and then stared down at the floor. "You have no idea."

"You said you shoved him in self-defense."

"I did." She looked warily at him. "That's not what I'm talking about."

He looked away, his attention landing on a little girl clutching a dirty rag doll with one hand, and the arm of an older woman with her other. Grady Memorial was a nightmare. On any given night, the trauma center was likely to have more shooting victims than they could handle and tonight was no exception.

"Evan?"

It was late. He was tired. More importantly, did he really want to hear what she had to say? He checked his watch and got to his feet. "It's after midnight. I'll drive you home."

"What about the hospital paperwork?" She got up, too, and put a hand on his arm. "Don't I have to sign something?"

"Are you two married?"

She blushed, and lowered her hand. "Of course not."

"Then you don't have to worry about it," he said, studying the way she tightly clasped her hands together. In spite of himself, he wondered what the hell this guy held over her.

"I guess not, but I am kind of responsible for—" She gave an angry shake of her head. "No, you're right. This isn't on me."

The place was so packed someone had already claimed their seats, and Evan motioned for her to precede him between the narrow rows of chairs. Besides, this was a hell of a place to be discussing anything so personal.

He watched her from behind, admiring how she'd dressed up in the off-the-shoulder sweater and silky pants. Had tonight gone as planned, they'd have had a nice dinner, gone to the concert and been in his bed by now. But that wasn't going to happen. Not tonight. Not ever again.

Neither spoke until they'd passed the sad-looking Christmas tree in the lobby near the exit doors. Then Liza said, "Thank you, Evan, for coming to my rescue tonight. For bringing me here. I don't know what I would've done without you."

"No problem." He couldn't look at her. Instead he busied himself with fishing his keys out of his pocket. Frankly, he would've preferred silence all the way back to her place. At this point, there wasn't anything she could say that would stop him from feeling like a chump. No matter which way he cut it, she'd used him.

"I know it's late—"

"Yep, and I have an early appointment tomorrow." Out of his peripheral vision he saw her turn sharply away.

"I need to talk to you," she said in a small voice he barely heard.

He paused, really tired all of a sudden. As if he'd been working a twenty-four-hour rotation. "I doubt there's anything to say."

Her laugh came out shaky. "I have so much to explain it could take the rest of the night."

Luckily, they got to his car quickly. He'd cheated and used the physician's parking area. Although he wasn't on staff here, tonight he figured he'd earned the spot. He unlocked the doors and, out of habit, he went around to open Liza's. Their eyes briefly meeting, a small regretful smile lifted the corners of her mouth before she got inside.

He went around the car, gulping in cold air. This would be a damn long ride to her place. If he'd been thinking straight, he would've called her a cab. Given her the money for the ride home. He'd done enough. Hell, who was he kidding? He could never have thrown her into a cab. Not tonight. Tomorrow was a different story.

He got behind the wheel, not knowing what to say. Nothing she could tell him would turn back time. The damage had been done. Maybe she'd figured that out for herself because she didn't say anything, either.

After they'd been on the road for about ten minutes, she said, "I can't imagine what's going through your mind right now, and I don't expect us to pick up where we left off…."

Man, she got that right.

"I'm not sure I'm entitled to even hope for forgiveness, but I have to explain what's behind all this."

He shook his head. "No, you don't."

"Evan…"

"You know what first attracted me to you?" he asked, keeping his eyes straight ahead. "You were refreshingly straightforward. You told it like it was. No games or bullshit."

"I am that person," she said softly. "This thing with Rick isn't just about me."

He shook his head as another thought occurred. With Rick out of the way, assuming she won the lawsuit, the money would be all hers. Evan exhaled sharply. Wow, he'd been such a damn fool.

"Please, Evan, I know an all-night coffee shop not far from here."

Right, so she could tell him more lies. Another block and they were at her apartment complex. He turned in and stopped in front of her building. "Good luck, Liza, I hope you get what you want."

He refused to look in her direction. He simply waited for her to get out, and then he sped away.

15

SHORTLY AFTER three-thirty that morning, sheer physical and mental exhaustion forced Liza to close her eyes. Sleep hadn't been soothing. Nightmares claimed her subconscious. Rick with his head bashed in and bleeding all over her. The police banging at her door. Handcuffs clamped around her wrists, while Eve and Jane stood off in the distance, laughing and pointing.

The most horrifying of all was the one where Evan sat on what appeared to be a throne, hovering several feet off the ground, watching her, shaking his head, tears brimming in his eyes. No matter how much she pleaded for him to listen, he said nothing and stared at her in abject disappointment.

Light had forced its way through the worn curtains before she opened her eyes again. She still lay on the couch where she'd collapsed after Evan had dropped her off. She still had on her clothes from last night and, fortunately, her watch. Feeling as if it weighed a ton, she lifted her wrist and squinted. It was already nine-forty.

The inside of her mouth was dry and nauseating,

reminding her that she hadn't even brushed her teeth. She pushed to her feet. Someone pounded at the door. Probably one of the neighbors, maybe even Mary Ellen. Ignoring them, she padded to the bathroom. Looking into the mirror was painful, so she lowered her head and got to the business of brushing her teeth and washing her face.

Next she'd call the hospital and check on Rick. She hoped he was okay. Maybe the frightening episode would wake him up and he'd get the help he needed. Astonishingly, the animosity she'd felt toward him for the past year had vanished. A calmness had eerily settled over her at some point last night.

Maybe it was because she was too drained to feel anything, or maybe it was the fact that she'd already made her decision to end the lawsuit and tell Eve and Jane everything…to not allow Rick to hold the diaries over her head like a club.

Eve and Jane would think she was insane for waiting until a week before the judge was supposed to hear the case. She'd put them through so much, but sadly, it had taken this long for Liza to swallow her pride, tell them the truth and ask for their help. Nearly a year of her life wasted because of pride.

All her life she'd handled everything herself. "Never risk disappointment by asking someone for help" was her motto. Ironic that she'd decided to tell Evan everything at dinner last night. Expose herself as the fool she'd been, and then if he wasn't totally disgusted with her, ask for his forgiveness. Too late now. Evan would never…

A sob swelled in her throat.

Damn, she couldn't get all soft and mushy now. She had a lot to do today. None of it pleasant. In the end, she'd feel better. And Eve and Jane would still hate her. And Evan…she could not go there.

She finished toweling off her face, and decided on making a couple of calls before taking a shower. Whoever had been knocking at the door was at it again. Great background noise for her phone calls.

Annoyed with the person's persistence, she didn't check the window to see who it was and jerked open the door. It was Mary Ellen, without Freedom. Thank God.

"I have been worried sick about you," the other woman said and walked past her into the apartment. She turned to face Liza, her eyes wide with a mixture of fear and relief. "What happened last night?"

Liza closed the door but didn't encourage Mary Ellen to advance into the apartment. "Rick overdosed."

"Is he okay?"

"He was last night. I was about to call the hospital to check on him."

"You looked awful when the ambulance came," Mary Ellen said, her face pale, the scar near her lip pronounced. "I thought you killed him."

"I bet everyone did."

Mary Ellen nodded.

Oddly, Liza didn't care. What did bother her was that she wouldn't have any money from the lawsuit to help Mary Ellen and her daughter. "Is Freedom okay?"

"Yep, she's in the playground. She thought you killed the stupid bastard, too."

"She didn't say it like that, I hope."

Mary Ellen vigorously shook her head. "She's a good girl."

"Yes, she is." Liza sighed. Somehow she had to help them. She'd be getting a job soon, and there was still about twenty-two-hundred dollars left of her inheritance in a savings account she'd squirreled away for an emergency. "Look, Mary Ellen," Liza said, her hand on the doorknob. "I have a lot to do today, but I'll see if I can pick up burgers for dinner."

"You don't have to do that."

"I know." She opened the door. "See you later, okay?"

"Good luck today," Mary Ellen said on her way out. After she stepped outside she turned back to Liza, and with a frown said, "You're different."

Liza smiled. "Actually, I feel like my old self for the first time in a year."

THE MIDTOWN ITALIAN restaurant, with its red-and-white checkered tablecloths and vases of fresh white daisies on each table, had once been a favorite of Eve, Jane and Liza's. Sitting as far back as she could, Liza waited for the other two to arrive, while mentally rehearsing what she was going to say to them.

It was simple, really. She'd tell them about Rick

having the diaries—the reason for the lawsuit—and that as of three hours ago, his doctor expected him to make a full recovery. He'd probably still want money in exchange for the diaries. Yep, real simple.

Sighing, she pushed aside the second cocktail napkin she'd shredded. The fact that they'd agreed to meet her and hadn't told her to go to hell was a good sign. After what they'd witnessed last night, pity alone could be the reason. But she'd accept any crumb they were willing to throw her. She owed them an explanation.

She saw Jane first, her hair so much blonder and longer now. Eve was right behind her, turning heads as they walked across the restaurant. Liza waved and they headed for her. Feeling awkward suddenly, she wished she'd had a glass of wine or something to calm the butterflies fluttering around in her stomach.

"Hello, Liza," Eve said first, while pulling out a chair.

"Hi." Jane looked uncomfortable.

"Thanks for coming," Liza said, despising how formal she sounded. "I'm sure you'd rather have told me to kiss off."

"That's not true," Jane said, claiming her seat. "I've missed you. We both have," she added, glancing at Eve, who busied herself with spreading the white linen napkin across her lap and refused to look up.

Liza smiled. Jane looked different, but she was still the same sweet woman who'd always been the one to smooth over the rough spots among the three of them. Eve was another story. Not that she hadn't always been a great friend, but she could be a tough cookie.

"So, what's on your mind?" an unsmiling Eve finally asked, with caution in her eyes.

Liza cleared her throat. "First, I want to apologize. I know that sounds weak. You both have every right to be furious with me. But I—" Her voice cracked. She cleared her throat again and then took a quick sip of water.

Neither woman spoke, but the compassion and hope she saw in their eyes gave her courage. The waitress came and took their drink orders, giving Liza another moment to compose herself.

"Eve, I did something horrible," she said the second the woman left. "I'm going to explain, but please don't get angry, just listen. I need to tell you this. It's important. For you."

Eve frowned. "I'm listening."

Liza took a deep breath. "Remember after your grandmother died, I offered to pack up her house?"

Eve slowly nodded.

"You asked me not to take Rick. I did anyway." Liza had loved Grammie as if she were her own grandmother. Not even Eve and Jane understood how devastating the woman's death had been for Liza. She'd been too good at playing tough. Letting everything roll off her back, including her parents' indifference toward her.

But when the time came to go to the old house belonging to the woman who'd made childhood bearable, Liza had crumbled like stale bread. She'd taken Rick with her for support. But that was no excuse, and she wouldn't use it now.

To her surprise, Eve's expression softened. "I should never have asked you to do that. It was selfish of me."

"No." Liza shook her head. "I was the selfish one. I failed you."

"You loved her, too, Liza," Eve said softly. "She was as much your grandmother as she was mine. You practically lived with us."

Liza had to blink back the emotion welling in her eyes. Eve understood about Grammie.

"Please tell me that's not what kept you away from us for the past year," Jane said, her expression horrified.

This was the hard part. Liza had to force herself to breathe. "There's more to it. Rick took something that belongs to you, Eve. I didn't know about it until…until a year ago."

The two women exchanged nervous glances, and then Eve asked, "What did he take?"

"Your diaries."

Eve slumped back and looking dazed. "The journals I started after my parents died," she said, more to herself. "How many did he take?"

"All of them."

"Oh, God." Jane covered her mouth.

Silence fell when the waitress returned with their drinks and set them down. They declined to order any food, and the woman left.

"There has to be a couple dozen notebooks," Eve said, her hand unsteady as she picked up her iced tea. "I stopped journaling right before we left for college."

"I didn't read anything," Liza assured her. "I didn't find out he took them until way after the fact." Seeing the fear in her friend's eyes, Liza wanted to cry, but that would do no good. "He wants money for them."

Eve's gaze narrowed before awareness dawned. "Is that what the lawsuit's about?"

Liza nodded.

"He's been blackmailing you?" Jane stared in disbelief. "This whole time?"

"Why didn't you come to us before now?" Eve asked, with so much hurt in her eyes that it left Liza cold.

"I was ashamed," Liza said quietly. "And I thought I could handle Rick, and that you would never need to know about any of it."

Eve stared down at her hand clutching the glass of iced tea. "So you just disappeared without a word."

"No, I was only supposed to be gone for a long weekend. To Atlantic City. Rick started losing money like crazy. After he drained my checking account and demanded more, I cut him off. I was going to leave him and catch the next flight back, and that's when he told me about the diaries."

"You should have at least called," Eve said, the fire back in her eyes. "It wasn't just about our friendship, you put the show in a bind."

"You're right. I have no excuse." She couldn't have called. Not without admitting what a fool she'd been and scare the hell out of Eve over the diaries, but she wasn't going to argue about that at this point. Pride had gotten her into enough trouble.

It didn't help that Eve seemed more concerned about Liza shunning them than she cared about the diaries. The thought made Liza sick to her stomach. How terribly foolish she'd been to not trust her friends.

Eve sighed. "Where's Rick now?"

"In the hospital."

"What happened?" Jane's eyes widened.

"I tried to kill him."

Both women gasped.

Liza gave them a wan smile. "He overdosed. Plus, he has a concussion from when I shoved him last night."

"You're not still with him, then," Jane said.

"God, no." Liza looked down, unable to meet their eyes. "Not really. But he's kept me on a short leash and I've allowed it. The show was really taking off, and when he threatened to sell the diaries to the tabloids I honestly didn't know what to do."

"You could've come to us. I thought that's what friends were for." The trace of bitterness in Eve's voice earned a sharp look from Jane.

"I know," Liza said quickly. "I was ashamed, and I honestly thought I could handle Rick. He needed money and I received a small inheritance from my father that I figured would—"

"I'm sorry. I didn't know. When did he pass away?" Eve asked, sincerity in her eyes.

"There was no love lost there."

"Still, I wish we'd known," Jane said softly.

Liza looked away. They'd been the best of friends, shared so many things, and she'd not only let them down, but had also held them at bay, making the occasional wisecrack about her parents but never letting them see how much she'd hurt. While they'd invited her into every aspect of their lives, she'd never totally let down her guard with them.

"My father was a lousy drunk," she said. "That's why there were never sleepovers at my house."

Eve smiled gently. "We knew that, Liza."

"No, I don't mean he got drunk once in a while, he was a drunken asshole six nights out of seven. Sometimes he'd hit my mother. Not me, not really, just the occasional slap, but that was probably because I wasn't around much."

Jane snorted. "We weren't stupid."

She looked closely into each of their faces. They did know. "You guys never said anything."

Eve shrugged. "What would that have changed?"

Liza's eyes burned. She did not want to cry now. She sniffed, cleared her throat. "Okay, here's the deal. I can withdraw the lawsuit and tell Rick to screw off but I have no idea how he'll react. I've looked everywhere I could think where he might hide the diaries and I've come up empty. Or we can see how the judgment plays out and if there's any money awarded, exchange it for the diaries."

Jane frowned. "Can't we go to the police?"

Liza shook her head. "We can't prove he stole them, or that he even has the diaries in his possession. Once he sells them to the tabloids, he's out of here."

They both looked at Eve, who'd remained silent. Finally, she said, "It's not fair to the others. They shouldn't have to pay blackmail money."

"I'm willing to give up half my share," Jane offered. "What about you, Eve?"

"Thanks, Jane, but I can't let you do that." Then, ignoring Jane's protest, Eve looked at Liza. "Would my share be enough? Would he take that?"

Liza looked at her friend, unable to stop the tears filling her eyes. What had she done? "I don't know. He should. That's all he would've gotten from the lawsuit."

"Liza, don't. It's okay." Eve left her chair to sit in the one next to Liza. She scooted it even closer, and then took Liza's hand. "It's only money. Not worth ruining our friendship. Do you hear me?"

The floodgates really opened then, and Liza grabbed a tissue out of her purse. "I've already done that. I've ruined everything."

"No, you haven't," Eve said, and Jane echoed her.

"You warned me Rick was scum, and I wouldn't listen."

"Like we ever thought you would have," Jane said.

Liza smiled, and dabbed at her cheeks. "You should've just hit me over the head."

"The thought crossed our minds." Eve squeezed her hand. "When is Rick getting out of the hospital?"

Liza hiccupped. "It'll be a while. He's going into detox first."

Eve nodded thoughtfully. "I think I should speak to my attorney about this before we do anything."

Jane nodded. "Eve, look at me."

At the firmness in Jane's voice, Eve and Liza both turned. She wasn't used to this new assertive Jane.

"I'm in this, too," Jane said. "I am giving half of my share, and it's not up for negotiation."

Eve rolled her eyes.

Liza sniffed. All she had to contribute was the problem itself. "I want you guys to know it really killed me to file the lawsuit," she whispered. "At the time, I didn't feel as if I had a choice. I'm so sorry."

"Forget it already." Eve smiled. "You know I'm not that famous. The tabloids might not even be interested in a bunch of teenage ramblings."

Jane and Liza exchanged looks. Yeah, right. First, she *had* become that famous, and second, what tabloid wouldn't love to take a shot at syndication's newest rising star?

"You remember writing anything too hot and heavy?" Liza asked.

Eve's smile vanished. "Right after my parents died I was pretty angry and bitter. Not very forgiving, either, as you well know." She exhaled slowly. "I doubt there would be anything in the diaries that would lastingly damage my career, but I won't lie,

I don't look forward to the humiliation of having my private thoughts and crazy teenage angst publicized."

"We won't let that happen," Liza said, aware that she hadn't done such a great job so far. "When I leave here I'm going to Rick's apartment and tear it apart. Without him looking over my shoulder I may be able to find a clue as to where he's keeping the diaries."

"I'll go with you," Jane said.

"Unfortunately, I have an important meeting with the network bigwigs in less than an hour." Eve glanced at her watch. "I'll be free this evening."

"That's okay," Liza said quickly. "I can do this by myself." The thought of Jane or Eve seeing the degrading way she'd lived for the past several months made her want to crawl into a ball and weep.

"I want to help," Jane insisted.

"Have I told you how terrific you look?" Liza asked, not just to distract her, which was part of it, but because Liza really meant it. "Your hair, your clothes, everything about you is really amazing."

Jane blushed. "I've been seeing this guy…."

"Anyone I know?"

Jane shook her head. "But I can't wait for you to meet him. His name's Perry."

While they talked, Eve's interested gaze stayed on Liza, her brows slightly furrowed as if she was obsessing over something that puzzled her. In the old days, Liza would've made a teasing remark. But not now, and it hurt so badly to realize that their once solid relationship was now too fragile for even the slightest misstep. All her own fault.

"So, Liza," Eve finally said, "tell us about Evan."

Hearing his name was all Liza needed to burst out into tears again.

16

AFTER SEARCHING Rick's apartment, Liza showered twice and still she felt his filth coating her skin. She'd filled three huge garbage bags of empty booze bottles and rotting food that, with the help of two guys working on a car, she hoisted into the Dumpster. She swore he hadn't washed his clothes or linen in months, and with total disgust she rummaged through each and every pocket, hoping for a clue as to the diaries' location. But she found nothing.

She'd worked at it well into the night, and eventually collapsed in exhaustion on her couch, too tired to even check out the refrigerator for a cola or some juice. Earlier Mary Ellen had knocked on the door and offered to make macaroni and cheese for dinner since Liza had totally forgotten to pick up burgers, but she wasn't in the mood to be around anyone. She wasn't only physically tired, her brain had gone in circles all day and had started to fizzle out.

Tomorrow was going to be a big day. She had to talk to Kevin Wade about withdrawing the lawsuit. That wouldn't be pleasant. He'd inevitably have questions she wouldn't want to answer. At least he'd already been paid. A total waste of money, but she'd already let that go. Then she had to talk to Rick.

The mere thought made her stomach roll. She hated seeing him, even more than she hated offering him one cent of Eve and Jane's winnings. And she wouldn't yet. First, she'd try and bluff him. He couldn't spend the money from prison, and she found enough heroin hidden in his apartment to put him away for a while. He'd been so messed up most of the time that he probably had forgotten his hiding places.

She realized the case could get sticky since she'd given him the money for the drugs, but at this point she didn't care. What did she have to lose? Not a damn thing. She'd already lost everything that mattered. Eve and Jane were still her friends, but they had to harbor some ill feelings. They were, after all, human.

Evan hated her. He had to.

She shuddered, thinking of the disappointment on his face. He'd made it clear that there was nothing she could tell him that would make a difference. He was right, of course, so she hadn't even bothered trying to call him.

But there was still this huge part of her that wanted to tell him she wasn't as bad as he thought she was. That she'd made foolish mistakes but her intention had been honorable. Even if he never wanted to speak to her again, did he have to think she was such an awful person?

Her cell phone rang, and damned if it wasn't sitting clear across the room. She struggled to her feet and reached it right before it would've gone to voice mail. It was Eve.

"Hey," Eve said as soon as Liza answered.

The casual familiarity of her voice had an amazingly emotional effect on Liza and it took her a second to compose herself. "Hey. Wish I had good news."

"No?"

"I searched places where no man or woman should have to go, especially without a tetanus shot. I found nothing. I'm sorry."

Eve paused. She had to be disappointed, but didn't let it show when she said, "You shouldn't have had to do that alone."

"Are you kidding? Do you remember who got us into this mess?"

"Knock that off. We're in this together, remember?"

"If you make me cry I'm gonna be so pissed off."

Eve laughed softly. "Have you been to the hospital yet?"

"No. That's tomorrow."

"Have you called Evan?"

Liza briefly closed her eyes. There were some things she didn't miss about having well-meaning but in-your-face friends. "That won't happen."

"Why not?"

"He doesn't want to talk to me, and I don't blame him."

"Okay, here's the problem…Nicole, the woman who took your place, she's leaving. Going home to California after the holidays. So if you're taking your old job back, you'll likely be bumping into—"

"Wait a minute."

"What?"

Liza's heart somersaulted. "Are you offering me my old job?"

"Yes, I am."

She heard the smile in Eve's voice, and dared to hope. Maybe there truly were no residual ill feelings. Well, that just made her feel worse. "I sued half the people associated with the show. I think that might be a little awkward."

"Maybe at first. But you are dropping the lawsuit and you're a damn good producer."

For one of the few times in her life, Liza didn't know what to say. She didn't deserve to have her old job back. Yet she wanted it with all her heart. "Have you discussed this with Jane and Cole and the others?"

"Of course Jane is over-the-moon excited at the prospect. Cole is the only other person with whom I've discussed this. He wants you back."

Cole Crawford was the supervising producer with whom she'd always gotten along, but he was also one of the lottery winners named in the lawsuit. "Seriously?"

"You'll make his job easier. He's also the only other person I told about the diaries. He even offered to kick in some money if it comes to that, which, of course, I wouldn't allow, but still that's Cole."

Liza swallowed around the lump in her throat. "I don't deserve any of you guys."

"Stop it already. Just say you'll come back."

"I want to. I do, but—"

"Then it's settled."

"If it causes any problems at all—"

"We'll address them at the time." Eve paused. "In the meantime, you should call Evan."

"Why?" Liza asked, although she knew where Eve was coming from. Working at the station, she was bound to occasionally run into Evan. The thought made her pulse quicken. Foolish to get excited, though. He thought she was scum.

Eve scoffed. "Don't be obtuse."

"He'll ignore me and that'll be fine."

"Liza."

"Look, Eve, I know you're trying to help, but trust me, I'm the last person in the world he wants to hear from. Leave it alone."

"If you don't quit being so damn hard on yourself, you'll never know, will you?"

Liza bit back a remark. "I'll think about it."

"Right. You do that." Eve paused, and Liza could hear someone talking in the background. "Look, you're off the hook for now. I've got to go."

Liza smiled. "Go."

She disconnected the call and got comfortable on the couch again. It wasn't about to be easy trying to slide back into her old life. There was bound to be resentment. And seeing Evan was going to be beyond horrible. But she wasn't about to pass up the opportunity to return to the best job she'd ever had or would ever have again.

Evan wouldn't be a problem. He'd be the perfect gentleman, smiling appropriately and greeting her in the halls, albeit briefly. An unknowing spectator wouldn't have a clue that there was bad blood between them.

She was the one who'd suffer, watching him, knowing she'd screwed things up, knowing she'd never again be in the arms of the best man she'd ever been with. And she'd deserve every last excruciating minute.

"THANK YOU FOR meeting with me. I really appreciate it," Eve said as soon as Evan walked into her office. "If you don't mind, would you close the door?"

Evan did as she asked and then sat down on the chair opposite her, the same chair he'd sat in last week when he'd come asking for her help. That was the only reason he was here now—to return the favor, even though any conversation about Liza was pointless. Two nights ago her actions had said it all. Nothing more to talk about.

"Would you like a cola or a bottle of water?" she asked.

"No, thank you. I only have a few minutes."

"Right." She smiled knowingly. "I won't take up much of your time."

As if on cue, his cell phone rang. "Excuse me, I have to take this." He looked at the caller ID. It was someone from Grady Memorial. Had to be about Rick, but why call him? He hesitated. This may not be a conversation he wanted to have in front of Eve.

"Do you need some privacy?" she asked.

"No, I'll return the call." He slipped the phone back into his pocket, curious as all get-out. "If this is about Liza, our conversation won't take long."

Eve looked at him hard. "I can't begin to imagine what you're thinking right now...."

"To tell you the truth, I've stopped thinking. Nothing to say, nothing to think about." He meant it. He'd beaten himself up enough for being a chump.

"I was there night before last. I saw what happened."

"You and everyone else."

Eve gave him a long, measuring look. "I hope this isn't about ego."

He laughed humorlessly. "She lied to me, and then she used me. Is that clear enough?"

Jerking her head back, she frowned. "How did she use you? She did no such thing."

He stared back at her, confused. "So now you're suddenly on her side?"

"I know Liza, and obviously she's done some stupid things, but she's never used anyone."

"You know what?" He got to his feet. "This is a complete waste of time."

"Wait, please. Let me explain something to

you, and then I swear I'll never say another word about Liza."

Between curiosity and the pleading in her green eyes, he stopped. How could she still defend the woman who'd betrayed her? "This better be good."

"Oh, it is." Eve gave him a weary smile. "Everything she's done in the past year, including filing the lawsuit, has been to protect me."

That got his attention. He sank back into the chair. "I'm listening."

EVAN THREW HIS CAR KEYS on the counter and went straight to the refrigerator. Usually he kept a six-pack in there in case Elton or Eric dropped by, but he couldn't remember what was left. Man, he sure could use a cold beer about now.

First, the meeting with Eve, and then the call from the E.R. nurse. His head hadn't stopped spinning since he left Grady Memorial an hour ago. He opened the refrigerator door and muttered a thanks. A lone green-tinted bottle sat on the top shelf. Perfect. He only needed one.

He uncapped the bottle and took it with him to the living room. Before he dropped onto the tan leather couch, he pulled the key the nurse had given him out of his pocket. It clearly belonged to a safe-deposit box. The nurse had found the key in Rick's sock the night he was admitted, and knew Evan had a keen interest in Rick's case. She'd taken a professional and ethical risk and called Evan. He'd promised her and her husband dinner, and against every grain of good sense and ethical bone in his body, he'd accepted the key.

The question was, what should he do with it? Give it to Eve? Or call Liza? He took a long cool sip of beer. After what Eve told him, he wanted to talk to Liza. He'd misjudged her. But she sure had helped feed his imagination. She could've explained about Rick, about the lawsuit. Yeah, he knew she'd tried, but only after the fact.

Hell, that was his ego talking. He'd wanted to rescue her. Be her knight in shining armor. He'd wanted to help solve her problems. But who the hell did he think he was? She hadn't turned to anyone for help, not even her best friends, women she'd grown up with. She'd wanted to handle her own mess. Call it pride or self-sufficiency. That's who Liza was. Take her or leave her.

She certainly didn't make it easy.

Shaking his head, he tipped the bottle to his lips. Less than two lousy weeks. That's all it had been since he'd really gotten to know her. How could he be in so emotionally deep? Was it because he'd finally caught the prize after admiring her from afar, or finally achieving success after having been shot down? He'd never been about the chase. Obviously, because even when he'd thought she'd used him, his feelings for her hadn't truly changed.

He'd been angry, mostly with himself, but that hadn't stopped him from wanting her, from lying awake thinking about how good it had been between them. That made him all the more an idiot.

Angela had taught him a valuable lesson—don't get emotionally involved. Don't be gullible. Have fun, be up front, have great sex. That's all. How often had he reminded himself? Yet when it came to Liza, his common sense took off in the wind.

He was glad Eve had told him about the diaries. As misguided as Liza had been, she'd tried to do what she thought was the right thing. Eve and Jane had forgiven her. She'd get back some of her old life. But that didn't mean everything would go back to the way it was between him and Liza. He didn't even know if she'd stay in Atlanta.

He laid his head back and swung his feet onto the oak coffee table, sending an old issue of *Psychology Today* flying across the room. He had to call Liza. Tell her about the key. It would be juvenile to ignore her and give it to Eve.

He mentally laughed at himself. As if he would deprive himself of the pleasure of delivering it to her. He still wanted to play the hero, wanted to see the look on Liza's face when he handed her the key and she realized he'd saved her ass.

He took a last gulp of beer and glanced at his watch. It wasn't too late. He'd go to her apartment. A block from there he'd call to tell her he was on his way. She'd wanted to explain about Rick, and Evan hadn't given her the chance. By now she might not even want to see him. Too bad.

He got up, jerked off his loosened tie and then dropped it on the couch. After leaving the empty bottle on the kitchen counter, he grabbed his keys and went out the back door. He hit the garage door button on the wall pad and as the door slid open, he got into his car. He put the car in Reverse and, waiting for the door to finish opening, his gaze went to the rearview mirror. A car pulled in behind him. It looked just like Liza's.

SHE SHOULD'VE CALLED. It was late, and what she had to say not only could've waited until tomorrow, but also until after Christmas, for that matter. But Liza wanted to see him. Had to see him. That is, if she ever wanted to get a good night's sleep again.

She squinted at the street sign on the right. Not that she'd ever paid much attention when she'd come to Evan's house before, but she was pretty sure that this was his street. She made the turn and saw the redbrick two-story house with the white gazebo that she'd noticed the morning he'd driven her to her car.

Nearly every house was decorated with colored lights strung along the eaves or woven through hedges and trees. The brick ranch-style house next to the two-story had a trio of animated reindeers sitting on the lawn, and the one after that had a large blow-up Santa swaying in the chilly breeze. Only two houses on the street were devoid of decorations. One of them belonged to Evan. She could see the starkness of it from half a block away.

She slowed the car down while her pulse sped up. He didn't want to see her. What if he refused to open the door? Just left her standing in the cold. No,

Evan was too much the gentleman. He'd let her in, listen to what she had to say and then throw her out. He'd be polite about it, of course, but there would be no mistake that he didn't want to see her again.

She squared her shoulders, and turned into his driveway. Admittedly, she'd been through worse. And she did have a perfectly legitimate reason for coming to talk to him. If she was going to be working for *Just Between Us* again and be at the studio every day, it was only right she warn him. Make sure they could be civil toward each other and not cause tension around the station.

That's what she'd told herself, anyway, when she'd been sitting in her apartment stewing over being unable to explain herself to him. He could listen for five crummy minutes. However, now that she was here, sitting in his driveway with the garage door slowly lifting, she wanted to get away as fast as she could. Although she just sat there, suddenly unsure.

Evan got out of his car first. Liza followed suit. They walked toward each other but he had the advantage of the garage light shining in her face. His was totally in shadow.

"Hi," he said. "I didn't expect you."

"I should've called."

"No, it's okay." He had on a white dress shirt, no tie and no suit jacket. Odd, because it was cold.

"If you're on your way out I can…" She cleared her throat, and took a step back. "I'll call you tomorrow."

"Why did you come?"

She hesitated. The gentleness in his voice unnerved her.

"It's business. Sort of."

"Yes?"

"First, I want to thank you for the other night and what you did for me. After that scene at the station…well, you could've told me to go to hell."

"No problem. I was doing my job."

"Speaking of jobs…" She cleared her throat. "I've been offered my old one." Damn, she wished she could see his face.

"Really?"

She sighed. He wasn't going to make this easy for her. "I know you can't forgive me for the other night, but I hope we can be civil."

"You're staying in Atlanta, then?"

"Yes."

He took a step closer, the streetlight illuminating his face. At the tenderness in his eyes her chest tightened. "Only for the job?"

"I don't deserve you, Evan." She probably would've run if fear and shock hadn't rooted her to the ground. He couldn't still want her. Was this some kind of cruel payback?

The corners of his mouth lifted ever so slightly. "Why not?"

"What do you mean?"

"That's a pretty strong opinion. I'd like to know how you arrived at it."

She glared at him. Why was he putting her on

the spot like this? "I never would've believed you had such a mean streak in you."

"Tell me why you don't think you deserve me."

"Damn you."

"Is it me? Or don't you think you deserve to be loved?" He must have realized she was about to take off. His hand darted out and he grabbed her wrist. "You want to keep running? How will that change anything? You'll only take the problem with you."

Liza tried to twist free but he wouldn't let her go. "Don't try and psychoanalyze me."

"No trying necessary. You lay it all out there." He pulled her closer. "Liza Skinner doesn't need anyone. She can take on the world. Translation—the further she keeps herself away from people, the less she'll get hurt." He hauled her up against him. "Guess what? I'm not going to let you get away with it anymore."

She had to tip her head back to look at him. She saw it then, the fierce determination in his eyes that told her he wasn't giving up on her. What a time to want to cry. She clung to him, blinking back the tears. She'd done too much crying in the past couple of days, more than in her entire adult life.

He brushed the back of his hand down her cheek. "Go ahead, let go," he whispered. "I've got you."

"And waste the moment?" Swallowing back the tears, Liza went up on tiptoes and touched his lips with hers. Softly, sweetly, letting him know how much he'd come to mean to her. How much she never wanted to let him down again. And then she kissed him like she never had before.

Epilogue

New Year's Day

THE PARTY TO CELEBRATE the recent distribution of the lottery money had already started by the time Evan and Liza entered the restaurant. The private back room where Eve and Jane and the rest of the staff had begun the festivities was buzzing with excitement. Liza looked forward to meeting some of the new members who had joined the show since she'd left. The initial sting of seeing everyone else was gone.

Between Eve and Jane and one too many Christmas parties, Liza was no longer persona non grata. Everyone who needed to know had been advised of the blackmail, but the details were kept to a minimum. Eve had welcomed her back with open arms and that seemed to be good enough for everyone else.

Christmas decorations were still up, and Liza whispered to Evan, "It'll be nice not to have all this stuff around, huh?"

He slid an arm around her shoulders. "Oh, I

don't know. I have a new perspective on Christmas."

She smiled. "Yeah?"

"Yep."

"Any particular reason why?" Making sure no one saw them, she brushed against his fly.

"You will pay for that." Stepping sway, he smiled at Eve, who waved them over to where she and Mitch and Jane and Perry were sipping champagne.

Liza laughed and linked an arm through his as they walked toward the group. The truth was, she'd also changed her mind about the holidays. How could she not after spending Christmas morning in front of the fireplace in bed with Evan? They'd barely made it to his parents' house in time for dinner.

"About time you two showed up," Eve said, waving an impatient hand. "Here." She passed them each a flute of the bubbly. Liza had already met Mitch and Perry, but Evan hadn't, so introductions were made.

"Nicole just informed me that she really doesn't want a going-away party so we're having a farewell toast soon," Eve said.

Liza said a silent thanks to Nicole, who was standing near the dessert table smiling at her significant other, Devon, who'd be going to California with her. Liza really didn't know Nicole, the woman who'd replaced her, but because she was leaving, Liza would be back at her old job tomorrow.

Cole Crawford, the show's supervising producer, walked up with his girlfriend, Jessie, and shook Evan's hand, and then kissed Liza on the cheek. "Where's Liza and what have you done with her?"

"Knock it off. You've seen me in a dress before."

"Once."

Liza frowned down at the simple-cut black dress that probably made her look way too thin. "No."

"Yes," Eve, Jane and Cole said at the same time.

"Okay, already."

Carrying drinks, Zach Haas and his girlfriend Kelly, an actress whom he met when she was a guest on the show, joined the group. Liza didn't really know Zach. He'd started with *Just Between Us* as a cameraman after she'd left. But she sheepishly recalled talking to him once when she'd wanted to pump him for information about the lawsuit.

"So," Evan said, "now that you all are filthy rich, what are your plans for the money?"

Zach laughed. "I don't know about filthy rich. I've always wanted to make a small indie film. That'll about wipe me out."

"Really?" Jane looked from him to Kelly. "You're exaggerating, I hope."

Kelly smiled fondly at him. "It's a huge risk, but he's going to do such an incredible job, he'll get his money back ten times over."

Conservative Jane frowned. Liza understood. Blowing all that money on one thing was scary. But she loved how Kelly supported Zach and his dream.

"What about you, Cole?" Liza asked. "I hope you don't have plans of retiring soon."

Eve scoffed. "He'd better not."

Smiling, Cole slipped an arm around Jessie. "We're taking the girls on one of those Disney cruise vacations," he said, referring to his twins, for whom he had sole custody. "And then we'll leave them with Annie and George while we tour Europe for three weeks."

Jessie beamed at him. "He's such a good guy, he's buying Annie a new car, too. But it's a surprise."

Cole looked embarrassed. "The rest goes into college funds. The little monkeys are growing so fast I can't keep up with them." He looked at Eve, clearly eager to redirect everyone's attention. "What about you?"

Eve glanced cryptically at Jane, whispered something to her date, Mitch, and then looked at Evan. "May we borrow her for a moment?"

Before Evan answered, Jane took one of Liza's arms and Eve took the other. They steered her to the far corner of the room away from everyone, and faced her.

"We have something to say and I'm warning you that this is not a negotiation." Eve had on her no-nonsense face. "Nor is it a request."

"Got it?" Jane added.

Startled, Liza nodded.

Eve reached into the small silver evening bag hanging over her shoulder. Jane's hand disappeared into a pocket of her blue silk dress. They exchanged pointed glances before each withdrew separate folded pieces of paper, and then at the same time, shoved each one into Liza's hands.

She looked down. It wasn't just paper. They each had given her a check. "What is this?" She unfolded one of them and nearly fell over at the sum.

"It's for you," Eve said. "Jane and I decided our shares should be split three ways."

Liza shook her head, and tried to give the checks back. "No way. I'm serious. No way."

Jane glared at her. "You wanna bet? Didn't Eve make it clear this is nonnegotiable?"

"You guys…" She couldn't accept this money. It wouldn't be fair. "If I cry and mess up my makeup, I'm gonna be really pissed."

"Tough." Jane wasn't having any of it.

Liza still hadn't gotten used to the change in her. "Seriously, this is such a nice gesture but—"

"Seriously…shut up," Eve insisted, "we have the diaries back and it didn't cost us a thing, thanks to Evan. Rick will not be seeing the outside of a jail cell for a while. Life is good. Enjoy."

Liza opened her mouth to protest further, but Jane cut her off. "Look, give some of the money to Mary Ellen, if it makes you feel better."

That got Liza's attention. She'd promised Mary Ellen that she'd help get her and Freedom out of that unsafe apartment complex. But that would have to wait until she got her first paycheck. The thing was, Liza was so broke that she could really use the money herself. Her pride told her to pass the checks back. It took every ounce of humility to keep them in her hand.

"Thank you," she whispered. "You guys are the best."

"Enough of that." Eve waved a hand. "Did you like Evan's parents? You went there for Christmas, yes?"

"Oh, here we go," Liza said, bracing herself to be interrogated. "Yes, they were very nice. Yes, Evan and I are talking about moving in together."

Jane let out a shriek that got everyone's attention. She briefly covered her mouth. "Sorry, but that is so cool."

Eve smiled, looking extraordinarily pleased. "He's a good man, Liza."

"You don't have to tell me that." Her gaze drifted toward him. He met her eyes and winked.

Neither of them looked away. How did she get so lucky? To have the best friends ever, and a guy she never dreamed could be so terrific. She hadn't told anyone yet, but she'd looked into trying a twelve-step meeting for adult children of alcoholics. If someone had suggested such a thing a year ago, she would've told them where to go. Not now. Evan meant too much to her. No way was she going to screw up this relationship.

She watched him say something to Mitch and Perry, and then head her way. As if they knew Liza needed a moment with him, Eve and Jane sort of drifted back to the guys.

Liza was standing alone when he reached her. He picked up her hand and kissed the back of it. "You are the most beautiful woman in this room, and I am the luckiest guy."

Readily, she stepped into his arms. "You couldn't be more mistaken, Evan," she whispered, tilting her head back for his kiss. "I'm the luckiest one by far."

* * * * *

Kimberley Blackstone didn't notice the waiting horde of media until it was too late. Flashbulbs exploded around her like a New Year's light show. She skidded to a halt, so abruptly her trailing suitcase all but overtook her.

This had to be a case of mistaken identity. Surely. Kimberley hadn't been on the paparazzi hit list for close to a decade, not since she'd estranged herself from her billionaire father and his headline-hungry diamond business.

But no, it was *her* name they called. *Her* face was the focus of a swarm of lenses that circled her like avid hornets. Her heart started to pound with fear-fueled adrenaline.

What did they want?

What was going on?

With a rising sense of bewilderment she scanned the crowd for a clue, and her gaze fastened on a tall, leonine figure forcing his way to the front. A tall, familiar figure. Her head came up in stunned recognition, and their gazes collided across the sea of heads before the cameras erupted with another barrage of flashes, this time right in her exposed face.

Blinded by the flashbulbs—and by the shock of that momentary eye-meet—Kimberley didn't realize his intent until he'd forged his way to her side, possibly by the sheer strength of his personality. She felt his arm wrap around her shoulder, pulling her into the protective shelter of his body, allowing her no time to object. No chance to lift her hands to ward him off.

In the space of a hastily drawn breath, she found herself plastered knee-to-nose against six feet two inches of hard-bodied male.

Ric Perrini.

Her lover for ten torrid weeks, her husband for ten tumultuous days.

Her ex for ten tranquil years.

After all this time, he should not have felt so familiar but, oh dear, he did. She knew the scent of that body and its lean, muscular strength. She knew its heat and its slick power and every response it could draw from hers.

She also recognized the ease with which he'd

taken control of the moment and the decisiveness of his deep voice when it rumbled close to her ear. "I have a car waiting outside. Is this your only luggage?"

Kimberley nodded. "I assume you will tell me," she said tightly, "what this welcome party is all about."

"Not while the welcome party is within earshot. No."

Barking a request for the cameramen to stand aside, Perrini took her hand and pulled her into step with his ground-eating stride. Kimberley let him, because he was right, damn his arrogant, Italian-suited hide. Despite the speed with which he whisked her across the airport terminal, she could almost feel the hot breath of the pursuing media on her back.

This was neither the time nor the place for explanations. Inside his car, however, she would get answers.

Now that the initial shock had been blown away—by the haste of their retreat, by the heat of her gathering indignation, by the rush of adrenaline fired by Perrini's presence and the looming verbal battle—her brain was starting to tick over. This had to be her father's doing. And if it was a Howard Blackstone publicity ploy, then it had to be about Blackstone Diamonds, the company that ruled his life.

The knowledge made her chest tighten with a familiar ache of disillusionment.

She'd known her father would be flying in from

Sydney for today's opening of the newest in his chain of exclusive, high-end jewelry boutiques. The opulent shop front sat adjacent to the rival business where Kimberley worked. No coincidence, she thought bitterly, just as it was no coincidence that Ric Perrini was here in Auckland ushering her to his car.

Perrini was Howard Blackstone's right-hand man, second in command at Blackstone Diamonds, a legacy of his short-lived marriage to the boss's daughter. No doubt her father had sent him to fetch her; the question was *why?*

* * * * *

*Get swept away down under with the glitz
and glamour of the Blackstone empire as
Kimberley tries to determine the real reason
behind her "reunion" with Ric....*

*Look for VOWS & A VENGEFUL GROOM
by Bronwyn Jameson,
in stores January 2008.*

REQUEST YOUR FREE BOOKS!

2 FREE NOVELS PLUS 2 FREE GIFTS!

HARLEQUIN®

Blaze®

Red-hot reads!

HB07

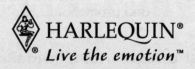

nocturne™

Jachin Black always knew he was an outcast.
Not only was he a vampire, he was a vampire
banished from the Sanguinas society. Jachin, forced
to survive among mortals, is determined to buy
his way back into the clan one day.

Ariel Swanson, debut author of a vampire novel, could
be the ticket he needs to get revenge and take his
rightful place among the Sanguinas again. However,
the unsuspecting mortal woman has no idea of the
dark and sensual path she will be forced to travel.

Look for

RESURRECTION: THE BEGINNING

by

PATRICE MICHELLE

Available January 2008 wherever you buy books.

Visit Silhouette Books at www.eHarlequin.com   SN61778

HARLEQUIN®

Blaze™

COMING NEXT MONTH

#369 ONE WILD WEDDING NIGHT Leslie Kelly
Blaze Encounters—One blazing book, five sizzling stories
Girls just want to have fun…. And for five bridesmaids, their friend's wedding night is the perfect time for the rest of them to let loose. After all, love is in the air. And so, they soon discover, is great sex…

#370 MY GUILTY PLEASURE Jamie Denton
The Martini Dares, Bk. 3
The trial is supposed to come first for the legal-eagle duo of Josephine Winfield and Sebastian Stanhope. But the long hours—and sizzling attraction—are taking their toll. Is it a simple case of lust in the first degree? Or dare she think there's more?

#371 BARE NECESSITIES Marie Donovan
A sexy striptease ignites an intense affair between longtime friends Adam Hale, a play-by-the-rules financial trader, and Bridget Weiss, a break-all-the-rules lingerie designer. But what will happen to their friendship now that their secret lust for each other is no longer a secret?

#372 DOES SHE DARE? Tawny Weber
Blush
When no-nonsense Isabel Santos decides to make a "man plan," she never dreams she'll have a chance to try it out with the guy who inspired it—her high school crush, hottie Dante Luciano. He's still everything she's ever wanted. And she'll make sure she's everything he'll *never* forget.…

#373 AT YOUR COMMAND Julie Miller
Marry in haste? Eighteen months ago Captain Zachariah Clark loved, married, then left Becky Clark. Now Zach's back home, and he's suddenly realized he knows nothing about his wife except her erogenous zones. Then again, great sex isn't such a bad place to start.…

#374 THE TAO OF SEX Jade Lee
Extreme
Landlord Tracy Williams wants to sell her building, almost as much as she wants her tenant, sexy Nathan Gao. But when Nathan puts a sale at risk by giving Tantric classes, Tracy has to bring a stop to them. That is, until he offers her some private *hands-on* instruction…

www.eHarlequin.com

HBCNM1207